Pearls ar

Raymond Cha to
England at an ollege,
completing his education in France and Germany.

In addition to his service with a Canadian infantry regiment in the First World War, he worked in many trades and professions – teacher, book reviewer, poet, paragraph writer, essayist, student pilot, accountant, oil executive and 'pulp' writer.

For the last forty years of his life he lived in the United States, largely in the Southern California region which provided the background for his classic series of Philip Marlowe crime novels. Raymond Chandler died in 1959.

Also by Raymond Chandler
in Pan Books

The High Window
The Little Sister
The Long Good-Bye
The Big Sleep
The Lady in the Lake
Playback
Smart-Aleck Kill

Raymond Chandler

Pearls are a Nuisance

Pan Books London and Sydney

The stories in this book are taken from *The Simple Art of Murder*

First published in Great Britain 1950 by Hamish Hamilton Ltd
This edition published 1980 by Pan Books Ltd,
Cavaye Place, London SW10 9PG
9 8 7 6 5 4 3 2

ISBN 0 330 26018 9
Printed and bound in Great Britain by
Hazell Watson & Viney Limited,
Member of the BPCC Group,
Aylesbury, Bucks

Contents

Introduction

Some literary antiquarian of a rather special type may one day think it worth while to run through the files of the pulp detective magazines which flourished during the late twenties and early thirties, and determine just how and when and by what steps the popular mystery story shed its refined good manners and went native. He will need sharp eyes and an open mind. Pulp paper never dreamed of posterity and most of it must be a dirty brown colour by now. And it takes a very open mind indeed to look beyond the unnecessarily gaudy covers, trashy titles and the barely acceptable advertisements and recognize the authentic power of a kind of writing that even at its most mannered and artificial made most of the fiction of the time taste like a cup of lukewarm consommé at a spinsterish tearoom.

I don't think this power was entirely a matter of violence, although far too many people got killed in these stories and their passing was celebrated with a rather too loving attention to detail. It certainly was not a matter of fine writing, since any attempt at that would have been ruthlessly blue-pencilled by the editorial staff. Nor was it because of any great originality of plot or character. Most of the plots were rather ordinary, and most of the characters rather primitive types of people. Possibly it was the smell of fear which the stories managed to generate. Their characters lived in a world gone wrong, a world in which, long before the atom bomb, civilization had created the machinery for its own destruction and was learning to use it with all the moronic delight of a gangster trying out his first machine-gun. The law was something to be manipulated for profit and power. The streets were dark with something more than night. The mystery story grew hard and cynical about motive and character, but it was not cynical about the effects it tried to produce nor about its technique for producing them. A few unusual critics recognized this at the time, which was all one had any right to expect. The average critic never recognizes an achievement when it happens. He explains it after it has become respectable.

The emotional basis of the standard detective story was and had always been that murder will out and justice will be done. Its technical basis was the relative insignificance of everything except the final dénouement. What led up to that was more or less passage-work. The dénouement would justify everything. The technical basis of the *Black Mask* type of story was that the scene outranked the plot in the sense that a good plot was one which made good scenes. The ideal mystery was one you would read if the end was missing. We who tried to write it had the same point of view as the film makers. When I first went to work in Hollywood a very intelligent producer told me that you couldn't make a successful motion picture from a mystery story, because the whole point was a disclosure that took a few seconds of screen time while the audience was reaching for its hat. He was wrong, but only because he was thinking of the wrong kind of mystery.

As to the emotional basis of the hard-boiled story, obviously it does not believe that murder will out and justice will be done – unless some very determined individual makes it his business to see that justice is done. The stories were about the men who made that happen. They were apt to be hard men and what they did, whether they were called police officers, private detectives or newspaper men, was hard, dangerous work. It was work they could always get. There was plenty of it lying around. There still is. Undoubtedly the stories about them had a fantastic element. Such things happened, but not so rapidly, nor to so close-knit a group of people, nor within so narrow a frame of logic. This was inevitable because the demand was for constant action; if you stopped to think you were lost. When in doubt, have a man come through a door with a gun in his hand. This could get to be pretty silly, but somehow it didn't seem to matter. A writer who is afraid to overreach himself is as useless as a general who is afraid to be wrong.

As I look back on my own stories it would be absurd if I did not wish they had been better. But if they had been much better they would not have been published. If the formula had been a little less rigid, more of the writing of that time might have survived. Some of us tried pretty hard to break out of the formula, but we usually got caught and sent back. To exceed the limits of a formula without destroying it is the dream of every magazine writer who is not a hopeless hack. There are things in my stories which I might like to change or leave out altogether. To do this may look simple, but if you try, you find you cannot do it at all. You will only destroy what is good without having any noticeable effect on what is bad. You cannot recapture the mood, the state of innocence, much less the animal gusto you had when you had very little else. Everything a writer learns about the art or craft of fiction takes just a little away from his need or desire to write at all. In the end he knows all the tricks and has nothing to say.

As for the literary quality of these exhibits, I am entitled to assume from the imprint of a distinguished publisher that I need not be sickeningly humble. As a writer I have never been able to take myself with that enormous earnestness which is one of the trying characteristics of the craft. And I have been fortunate to escape what has been called (by *Punch*, I think) 'that form of snobbery which can accept the Literature of Entertainment in the Past, but only the Literature of Enlightenment in the Present'. Between the one-syllable humours of the comic strip and the anaemic subleties of the littérateurs there is a wide stretch of country, in which the mystery story may or may not be an important landmark. There are those who hate it in all its forms. There are those who like it when it is about nice people ('that charming Mrs Jones, whoever would have thought she would cut off her husband's head with a meat saw? Such a handsome man, too!'). There are those who think violence and sadism interchangeable terms, and those who regard detective fiction as sub-literary on no better grounds than that it does not habitually get itself jammed up with subordinate clauses, tricky punctuation and hypothetical subjunctives. There are those who read it only when they are tired or sick, and from the number of mystery novels they consume they must be tired or sick most of the time. There are the aficionados of deduction (with whom I have had words elsewhere) and the aficionados of sex who can't get it into their hot little heads that the fictional detective is a catalyst not a Casanova. The former demand a ground plan of Greythorpe Manor, showing the study, the gun-room, the main hall and staircase and the passage to that grim little room where the butler polishes the Georgian silver, thin-lipped and silent, hearing the murmur of doom. The latter think the shortest distance between two points is from a blonde to a bed.

No writer can please them all, no writer should try. The stories in this book certainly had no thought of being able to please anyone ten years after they were written. The mystery story is a kind of writing that need not dwell in the shadow of the past and owes little if any allegiance to the cult of the classics. It is a good deal more than unlikely that any writer now living will produce a better historical novel than *Henry Esmond*, a better tale of children than *The Golden Age*, a sharper social vignette than *Madame Bovary*, a more graceful and elegant evocation than *The Spoils of Poynton*, a wider and richer canvas than *War and Peace* or *The Brothers Karamazov*. But to devise a more plausible mystery than *The Hound of the Baskervilles* or *The Purloined Letter* should not be too difficult. Nowadays it would be rather more difficult not to. There are no 'classics' of crime and detection. Not one. Within its frame of reference, which is the only way it should be judged, a classic is a piece of writing which exhausts the possibilities of its form and can never be surpassed. No story or novel of mystery has done that yet. Few have come close. Which is one of the principal reasons why otherwise reasonable people continue to assault the citadel.

Raymond Chandler

Pearls are a Nuisance

It is quite true that I wasn't doing anything that morning except looking at a blank sheet of paper in my typewriter and thinking about writing a letter. It is also quite true that I don't have a great deal to do any morning. But that is no reason why I should have to go out hunting for old Mrs Penruddock's pearl necklace. I don't happen to be a policeman.

It was Ellen Macintosh who called me up, which made a difference, of course. 'How are you, darling?' she asked. 'Busy?'

'Yes and no,' I said. 'Mostly no. I am very well. What is it now?'

'I don't think you love me, Walter. And anyway you ought to get some work to do. You have too much money. Somebody has stolen Mrs Penruddock's pearls and I want you to find them.'

'Possibly you think you have the police department on the line,' I said coldly. 'This is the residence of Walter Gage. Mr Gage talking.'

'Well, you can tell Mr Gage from Miss Ellen Macintosh,' she said, 'that if he is not out here in half an hour, he will receive a small parcel by registered mail containing one diamond engagement ring.'

'And a lot of good it did me,' I said. 'That old crow will live for another fifty years.'

But she had already hung up so I put my hat on and went down and drove off in the Packard. It was a nice late April morning, if you care for that sort of thing. Mrs Penruddock lived on a wide quiet street in Carondelet Park. The house had probably looked exactly the same for the last fifty years, but that didn't make me any better pleased that Ellen Macintosh might live in it another fifty years, unless old Mrs Penruddock died and didn't need a nurse any more. Mr Penruddock had died a few years before, leaving no will, a thoroughly tangled-up estate, and a list of pensioners as long as a star boarder's arm.

I rang the front doorbell and the door was opened, not very soon, by a little old woman with a maid's apron and a strangled knot of grey hair on the top of her head. She looked at me as if she had never seen me before and didn't want to see me now.

'Miss Ellen Macintosh, please,' I said. 'Mr Walter Gage calling.'

She sniffed, turned without a word and we went back into the musty recesses of the house and came to a glassed-in porch full of wicker furniture and the smell of Egyptian tombs. She went away, with another sniff.

In a moment the door opened again and Ellen Macintosh came in. Maybe you don't like tall girls with honey-coloured hair and skin like the first strawberry peach the grocer sneaks out of the box for himself. If you don't, I'm sorry for you.

'Darling, so you did come,' she cried. 'That was nice of you, Walter. Now sit down and I'll tell you all about it.'

We sat down.

'Mrs Penruddock's pearl necklace has been stolen, Walter.'

'You told me that over the telephone. My temperature is still normal.'

'If you will excuse a professional guess,' she said, 'it is probably subnormal – permanently. The pearls are a string of forty-nine matched pink ones which Mr Penruddock gave to Mrs Penruddock for her golden wedding present. She hardly ever wore them lately, except perhaps at Christmas or when she had a couple of very old friends in to dinner and was well enough to sit up. And every Thanksgiving she gives a dinner to all the pensioners and friends and old employees Mr Penruddock left on her hands, and she wore them then.'

'You are getting your verb tenses a little mixed,' I said, 'but the general idea is clear. Go on.'

'Well, Walter,' Ellen said, with what some people call an

arch look, 'the pearls have been stolen. Yes, I know that is the third time I told you that, but there's a strange mystery about it. They were kept in a leather case in an old safe which was open half the time and which I should judge a strong man could open with his fingers even when it was locked. I had to go there for a paper this morning and I looked in at the pearls just to say hello—'

'I hope your idea in hanging on to Mrs Penruddock has not been that she might leave you that necklace,' I said stiffly. 'Pearls are all very well for old people and fat blondes, but for tall willowy—'

'Oh shut up, darling,' Ellen broke in. 'I should certainly not have been waiting for these pearls – because they were false.'

I swallowed hard and stared at her. 'Well,' I said, with a leer, 'I have heard that old Penruddock pulled some cross-eyed rabbits out of the hat occasionally, but giving his own wife a string of phoney pearls on her golden wedding gets my money.'

'Oh, don't be such a fool, Walter! They were real enough then. The fact is Mrs Penruddock sold them and had imitations made. One of her old friends, Mr Lansing Gallemore of the Gallemore Jewellery Company, handled it all for her very quietly, because of course she didn't want anyone to know. And that is why the police have not been called in. You *will* find them for her, won't you, Walter?'

'How? And what did she sell them for?'

'Because Mr Penruddock died suddenly without making any provision for all these people he had been supporting. Then the depression came, and there was hardly any money at all. Only just enough to carry on the household and pay the servants, all of whom have been with Mrs Penruddock so long that she would rather starve than let any of them go.'

'That's different,' I said. 'I take my hat off to her. But how the dickens am I going to find them, and what does it matter anyway – if they were false?'

'Well, the pearls – imitations, I mean – cost two hundred dollars and were specially made in Bohemia and it took several months and the way things are over there now she might never be able to get another set of really good imitations. And she is terrified somebody will find out they were false, or that the thief will blackmail her, when he finds out they were false. You see, darling, I know who stole them.'

I said, 'Huh?' a word I very seldom use as I do not think it part of the vocabulary of a gentleman.

'The chauffeur we had here a few months, Walter – a horrid big brute named Henry Eichelberger. He left suddenly the day before yesterday, for no reason at all. Nobody ever leaves Mrs Penruddock. Her last chauffeur was a very old man and he died. But Henry Eichelberger left without a word and I'm sure he had stolen the pearls. He tried to kiss me once, Walter.'

'Oh, he did,' I said in a different voice. 'Tried to kiss you, eh? Where is this big slab of meat, darling? Have you any idea at all? It seems hardly likely he would be hanging around on the street corner for me to punch his nose for him.'

Ellen lowered her long silky eyelashes at me – and when she does that I go limp as a scrubwoman's back hair.

'He didn't run away. He must have known the pearls were false and that he was safe enough to blackmail Mrs Penruddock, I called up the agency he came from and he has been back there and registered again for employment. But they said it was against their rules to give his address.'

'Why couldn't somebody else have taken the pearls? A burglar, for instance?'

'There is no one else. The servants are beyond suspicion and the house is locked up as tight as an icebox every night and there were no signs of anybody having broken in. Besides Henry Eichelberger knew where the pearls were kept, because he saw me putting them away after the last time she wore them – which was when she had two very dear friends in to dinner on the occasion of the anniversary of Mr Penruddock's death.'

'That must have been a pretty wild party,' I said. 'All right, I'll go down to the agency and make them give me his address. Where is it?'

'It is called the Ada Twomey Domestic Employment Agency, and it is in the two-hundred block on East Second, a very unpleasant neighbourhood.'

'Not half as unpleasant as my neighbourhood will be to Henry Eichelberger,' I said. 'So he tried to kiss you, eh?'

'The pearls, Walter,' Ellen said gently, 'are the important thing. I do hope he hasn't already found out they are false and thrown them in the ocean.'

'If he has, I'll make him dive for them.'

'He is six feet three and very big and strong, Walter,' Ellen said coyly. 'But not handsome like you, of course.'

'Just my size,' I said. 'It will be a pleasure. Good-bye, darling.'

She took hold of my sleeve. 'There is just one thing, Walter. I don't mind a little fighting because it is manly. But you mustn't cause a disturbance that would bring the police in, you know. And although you are very big and strong and played right tackle at college, you are a little weak about one thing. Will you promise me not to drink any whisky?'

'This Eichelberger,' I said, 'is all the drink I want.'

Two

The Ada Twomey Domestic Employment Agency on East Second Street proved to be all that the name and location implied. The odour of the anteroom, in which I was compelled to wait for a short time, was not at all pleasant. The agency was presided over by a hard-faced middle-aged woman who said that Henry Eichelberger was registered with them for employment as a chauffeur, and that she could arrange to have him call upon me, or could bring him there to the office for an interview. But when I placed a ten-dollar bill on her desk and indicated that it was merely an earnest of good faith, without prejudice to any commission which might become due to her agency, she relented and gave me his address, which was out west on Santa Monica Boulevard, near the part of the city which used to be called Sherman.

I drove out there without delay, for fear that Henry Eichelberger might telephone in and be informed that I was coming. The address proved to be a seedy hotel, conveniently close to the interurban car tracks and having its entrance adjoining a Chinese laundry. The hotel was upstairs, the steps being covered – in places – with strips of decayed rubber matting to which were screwed irregular fragments of unpolished brass. The smell of the Chinese laundry ceased about halfway up the stairs and was replaced by a smell of kerosene, cigar butts, slept-in air and greasy paper bags. There was a register at the head of the stairs on a wooden shelf. The last entry was in pencil, three weeks previous as to date, and had been written by someone with a very unsteady hand. I deduced from this that the management was not over-particular.

There was a bell beside the book and a sign reading: MANAGER. I rang the bell and waited. Presently a door opened down the hall and feet shuffled towards me without haste. A man appeared wearing frayed leather slippers and trousers of a nameless colour, which had the two top buttons unlatched to permit more freedom to the suburbs of his extensive stomach. He also wore red suspenders, his shirt was darkened under the arms, and elsewhere, and his face badly needed a thorough laundering and trimming.

He said, 'Full up, bud,' and sneered.

I said: 'I am not looking for a room. I am looking for one Eichelberger, who, I am informed lives here, but who, I observe, has not registered in your book. And this, as of course you know, is contrary to the law.'

'A wise guy,' the fat man sneered again. 'Down the hall,

bud. Two-eighteen.' He waved a thumb the colour and almost the size of a burnt baked potato.

'Have the kindness to show me the way,' I said.

'Geez, the lootenant-governor,' he said, and began to shake his stomach. His small eyes disappeared in folds of yellow fat. 'Okay, bud. Follow on.'

We went into the gloomy depths of the back hall and came to a wooden door at the end with a closed wooden transom above it. The fat man smote the door with a fat hand. Nothing happened.

'Out,' he said.

'Have the kindness to unlock the door,' I said. 'I wish to go in and wait for Eichelberger.'

'In a pig's valise,' the fat man said nastily. 'Who the hell you think you are, bum?'

This angered me. He was a fair-sized man, about six feet tall, but too full of the memories of beer. I looked up and down the dark hall. The place seemed utterly deserted.

I hit the fat man in the stomach.

He sat down on the floor and belched and his right knee-cap came into sharp contact with his jaw. He coughed and tears welled up in his eyes.

'Cripes, bud,' he whined. 'You got twenty years on me. That ain't fair.'

'Open the door,' I said. 'I have no time to argue with you.'

'A buck,' he said, wiping his eyes on his shirt. 'Two bucks and no tip-off.'

I took two dollars out of my pocket and helped the man to his feet. He folded the two dollars and produced an ordinary pass-key which I could have purchased for five cents.

'Brother, you sock,' he said. 'Where you learn it? Most big guys are muscle-bound.' He unlocked the door.

'If you hear any noises later on,' I said, 'ignore them. If there is any damage, it will be paid for generously.'

He nodded and I went into the room. He locked the door behind me and his steps receded. There was silence.

The room was small, mean and tawdry. It contained a

brown chest of drawers with a small mirror hanging over it, a straight wooden chair, a wooden rocking chair, a single-bed of chipped enamel, with a much mended cotton counterpane. The curtains at the single window had fly marks on them and the green shade was without a slat at the bottom. There was a washbowl in the corner with two paper-thin towels hanging beside it. There was, of course, no bathroom, and there was no closet. A piece of dark figured material hanging from a shelf made a substitute for the latter. Behind this I found a grey business suit of the largest size made, which would be my size, if I wore ready-made clothes, which I do not. There was a pair of black brogues on the floor, size number twelve at least. There was also a cheap fibre suitcase, which of course I searched, as it was not locked.

I also searched the bureau and was surprised to find that everything in it was neat and clean and decent. But there was not much in it. Particularly there were no pearls in it. I searched in all other likely and unlikely places in the room but I found nothing of interest.

I sat on the side of the bed and lit a cigarette and waited. It was now apparent to me that Henry Eichelberger was either a very great fool or entirely innocent. The room and the open trail he had left behind him did not suggest a man dealing in operations like stealing pearl necklaces.

I had smoked four cigarettes, more than I usually smoke in an entire day, when approaching steps sounded. They were light quick steps but not at all clandestine. A key was thrust into the door and turned and the door swung carelessly open. A man stepped through it and looked at me.

I am six feet three inches in height and weigh over two hundred pounds. This man was tall, but he seemed lighter. He wore a blue serge suit of the kind which is called neat for lack of anything better to say about it. He had thick wiry blond hair, a neck like a Prussian corporal in a cartoon, very wide shoulders and large hard hands, and he had a face that had taken much battering in its time. His small greenish eyes glinted at me with what I then took to be evil humour. I saw at once that he was not a man to trifle with, but I was not afraid of him. I was his equal in size and strength, and, I had small doubt, his superior in intelligence.

I stood up off the bed calmly and said: 'I am looking for one Eichelberger.'

'How you get in here, bud?' It was a cheerful voice, rather heavy, but not unpleasant to the ear.

'The explanation of that can wait,' I said stiffly. 'I am looking for one Eichelberger. Are you he?'

'Haw,' the man said. 'A gut-buster. A comedian. Wait'll I loosen my belt.' He took a couple of steps farther into the room and I took the same number towards him.

'My name is Walter Gage,' I said. 'Are you Eichelberger?'

'Gimme a nickel,' he said, 'and I'll tell you.'

I ignored that. 'I am the fiancé of Miss Ellen Macintosh,' I told him coldly. 'I am informed that you tried to kiss her.'

He took another step towards me and I another towards him. 'Whaddaya mean – tried?' he sneered.

I led sharply with my right and it landed flush on his chin. It seemed to me a good solid punch, but it scarcely moved him. I then put two hard left jabs into his neck and landed a second hard right at the side of his rather wide nose. He snorted and hit me in the solar plexus.

I bent over and took hold of the room with both hands and spun it. When I had it nicely spinning I gave it a full swing and hit myself on the back of the head with the floor. This made me lose my balance temporarily and while I was thinking about how to regain it a wet towel began to slap at my face and I opened my eyes. The face of Henry Eichelberger was close to mine and bore a certain appearance of solicitude.

'Bud,' his voice said, 'your stomach is as weak as a Chinaman's tea.'

'Brandy!' I croaked. 'What happened?'

'You tripped on a little bitty tear in the carpet, bud. You really got to have liquor?'

'Brandy,' I croaked again, and closed my eyes.

'I hope it don't get me started,' his voice said.

A door opened and closed. I lay motionless and tried to avoid being sick at my stomach. The time passed slowly, in a long grey veil. Then the door of the room opened and closed once more and a moment later something hard was being pressed against my lips. I opened my mouth and liquor poured down my throat. I coughed, but the fiery liquid coursed through my veins and strengthened me at once. I sat up.

'Thank you, Henry,' I said. 'May I call you Henry?'

'No tax on it, bud.'

I got to my feet and stood before him. He stared at me curiously. 'You look okay,' he said. 'Why'n't you told me you was sick?'

'Damn you, Eichelberger!' I said and hit with all my strength on the side of his jaw. He shook his head and his eyes seemed annoyed. I delivered three more punches to his face and jaw while he was still shaking his head.

'So you wanta play for keeps!' he yelled and took hold of the bed and threw it at me.

I dodged the corner of the bed, but in doing so I moved a little too quickly and lost my balance and pushed my head about four inches in the baseboard under the window.

A wet towel began to slap at my face. I opened my eyes.

'Listen, kid. You got two strikes and no balls on you. Maybe you oughta try a lighter bat.'

'Brandy,' I croaked.

'You'll take rye.' He pressed a glass against my lips and I drank thirstily. Then I climbed to my feet again.

The bed, to my astonishment, had not moved. I sat down on it and Henry Eichelberger sat down beside me and patted my shoulder.

'You and me could get along,' he said. 'I never kissed your girl, although I ain't saying I wouldn't like to. Is that all is worrying at you?'

He poured himself half a waterglassful of the whisky out of the pint bottle which he had gone out to buy. He swallowed the liquor thoughtfully.

'No, there is another matter,' I said.

'Shoot. But no more haymakers. Promise?'

I promised him rather reluctantly. 'Why did you leave the employ of Mrs Penruddock?' I asked him.

He looked at me from under his shaggy blond eyebrows. Then he looked at the bottle he was holding in his hand. 'Would you call me a looker?' he asked.

'Well, Henry—'

'Don't pansy up on me,' he snarled.

'No, Henry, I should not call you very handsome. But unquestionably you are virile.'

He poured another half-waterglassful of whisky and handed it to me. 'Your turn,' he said. I drank it down without fully realizing what I was doing. When I had stopped coughing Henry took the glass out of my hand and refilled it. He took his own drink moodily. The bottle was now nearly empty.

'Suppose you fell for a dame with all the looks this side of heaven. With a map like mine. A guy like me, a guy from the stockyards that played himself a lot of very tough left end at a cow college and left his looks and education on the scoreboard. A guy that has fought everything but whales and freight hogs – engines to you – and licked 'em all, but naturally had to take a sock now and then. Then I get a job where I see this lovely all the time and every day and know it's no dice. What would you do, pal? Me, I just quit the job.'

'Henry, I'd like to shake your hand,' I said.

He shook hands with me listlessly. 'So I ask for my time,' he said. 'What else would I do?' He held the bottle up and looked at it against the light. 'Boy, you made an error when you had me get this. When I start drinking it's a world cruise. You got plenty dough?'

'Certainly,' I said. 'If whisky is what you want, Henry, whisky is what you shall have. I have a very nice apartment on Franklin Avenue in Hollywood and while I cast no aspersions on your own humble and of course quite temporary abode, I now suggest we repair to my apartment, which is a good deal larger and gives one more room to extend one's elbow.' I waved my hand airily.

'Say, you're drunk,' Henry said, with admiration in his small green eyes.

'I am not yet drunk, Henry, although I do in fact feel the effect of that whisky and very pleasantly. You must not mind my way of talking which is a personal matter, like your own clipped and concise method of speech. But before we depart there is one other rather insignificant detail I wish to discuss with you. I am empowered to arrange for the return of Mrs Penruddock's pearls. I understand there is some possibility that you may have stolen them.'

'Son, you take some awful chances,' Henry said softly.

'This is a business matter, Henry, and plain talk is the best way to settle it. The pearls are only false pearls, so we should very easily be able to come to an agreement. I mean you no ill will, Henry, and I am obliged to you for procuring the whisky, but business is business. Will you take fifty dollars and return the pearls and no questions asked?'

Henry laughed shortly and mirthlessly, but he seemed to have no animosity in his voice when he said: 'So you think I stole some marbles and am sitting around here waiting for a flock of dicks to swarm me?'

'No police have been told, Henry, and you may not have known the pearls were false. Pass the liquor, Henry.'

He poured me most of what was left in the bottle, and I drank it down with the greatest good humour. I threw the glass at the mirror, but unfortunately missed. The glass, which was of heavy and cheap construction, fell on the floor and did not break. Henry Eichelberger laughed heartily.

'What are you laughing at, Henry?'

'Nothing,' he said. 'I was just thinking what a sucker some guy is finding out he is – about them marbles.'

'You mean you did not steal the pearls, Henry?'

He laughed again, a little gloomily. 'Yeah,' he said, 'meaning no. I oughta sock you, but what the hell? Any guy can get a bum idea. No, I didn't steal no pearls, bud. If they was ringers, I wouldn't be bothered, and if they was what they looked like the one time I saw them on the old lady's neck,

I wouldn't decidedly be holed up in no cheap flop in LA waiting for a couple carloads of johns to put the sneeze on me.'

I reached for his hand again and shook it.

'That is all I required to know,' I said happily. 'Now I am at peace. We shall now go to my apartment and consider ways and means to recover these pearls. You and I together should make a team that can conquer any opposition, Henry.'

'You ain't kidding me, huh?'

I stood up and put my hat on – upside down. 'No, Henry. I am making you an offer of employment which I understand you need, and all the whisky you can drink. Let us go. Can you drive a car in your condition?'

'Hell, I ain't drunk,' Henry said, looking surprised.

We left the room and walked down the dark hallway. The fat manager very suddenly appeared from some nebulous shade and stood in front of us rubbing his stomach and looking at me with small greedy expectant eyes. 'Everything oke?' he inquired, chewing on a time-darkened toothpick.

'Give him a buck,' Henry said.

'What for, Henry?'

'Oh, I dunno. Just give him a buck.'

I withdrew a dollar bill from my pocket and gave it to the fat man.

'Thanks, pal,' Henry said. He chucked the fat man under the Adam's apple, and removed the dollar bill deftly from between his fingers. 'That pays for the hooch,' he added. 'I hate to have to bum dough.'

We went down the stairs arm in arm, leaving the manager trying to cough the toothpick up from his oesophagus.

Three

At five o'clock that afternoon I awoke from slumber and found that I was lying on my bed in my apartment in the Château Moraine, on Franklin Avenue near Ivar Street, in Hollywood. I turned my head, which ached, and saw that Henry Eichelberger was lying beside me in his undershirt and trousers. I then perceived that I also was as lightly attired. On the table near by there stood an almost full bottle of Old Plantation rye whisky, the full quart size, and on the floor lay an entirely empty bottle of the same excellent brand. There were garments lying here and there on the floor, and a cigarette had burned a hole in the brocaded arm of one of my easy chairs.

I felt myself over carefully. My stomach was stiff and sore and my jaw seemed a little swollen on one side. Otherwise I was none the worse for wear. A sharp pain darted through my temples as I stood up off the bed, but I ignored it and walked steadily to the bottle on the table and raised it to my lips. After a steady draught of the fiery liquid I suddenly felt much better. A hearty and cheerful mood came over me and I was ready for any adventure. I went back to the bed and shook Henry firmly by the shoulder.

'Wake up, Henry,' I said. 'The sunset hour is nigh. The robins are calling and the squirrels are scolding and the morning glories furl themselves in sleep.'

Like all men of action Henry Eichelberger came awake with his fist doubled. 'What was that crack?' he snarled. 'Oh, yeah. Hi, Walter. How you feel?'

'I feel splendid. Are you rested?'

'Sure.' He swung his shoeless feet to the floor and rumpled his thick blond hair with his fingers. 'We was going swell until you passed out,' he said. 'So I had me a nap. I never drink solo. You okay?'

'Yes, Henry, I feel very well indeed. And we have work to do.'

'Swell.' He went to the whisky bottle and quaffed from it freely. He rubbed his stomach with the flat of his hand. His green eyes shone peacefully. 'I'm a sick man,' he said, 'and I got to take my medicine.' He put the bottle down on the table and surveyed the apartment. 'Geez,' he said, 'we thrown it into us so fast I ain't hardly looked at the dump. You got a nice little place here, Walter. Geez, a white typewriter and a white telephone. What's the matter, kid – you just been confirmed?'

'Just a foolish fancy, Henry,' I said, waving an airy hand.

Henry went over and looked at the typewriter and the telephone side by side on my writing desk, and the silver-mounted desk set, each piece chased with my initials.

'Well fixed, huh?' Henry said, turning his green gaze on me.

'Tolerably so, Henry,' I said modestly.

'Well, what next, pal? You got any ideas or do we just drink some?'

'Yes, Henry, I do have an idea. With a man like you to help me I think it can be put into practice. I feel that we must, as they say, tap the grapevine. When a string of pearls is stolen, all the underworld knows it at once. Pearls are hard to sell, Henry, inasmuch as they cannot be cut and can be identified by experts, I have read. The underworld will be seething with activity. It should not be too difficult for us to find someone who would send a message to the proper quarter that we are willing to pay a reasonable sum for their return.'

'You talk nice – for a drunk guy,' Henry said, reaching for the bottle. 'But ain't you forgot these marbles are phonies?'

'For sentimental reasons I am quite willing to pay for their return, just the same.'

Henry drank some whisky, appeared to enjoy the flavour of it and drank some more. He waved the bottle at me politely.

'That's okay – as far as it goes,' he said. 'But this underworld that's doing all this here seething you spoke of ain't going to seethe a hell of a lot over a string of glass beads. Or am I screwy?'

'I was thinking, Henry, that the underworld probably has a sense of humour and the laugh that would go around would be quite emphatic.'

'There's an idea in that,' Henry said. 'Here's some mug finds out lady Penruddock has a string of oyster fruit worth oodles of kale, and he does hisself a neat little box job and torts down to the fence. And the fence gives him the belly laugh. I would say something like that could get around the poolrooms and start a little idle chatter. So far, so nutty. But this box man is going to dump them beads in a hurry, because he has a three-to-ten on him even if they are only worth a nickel plus sales tax. Breaking and entering is the rap, Walter.'

'However, Henry,' I said, 'there is another element in the situation. If this thief is very stupid, it will not, of course, have much weight. But if he is even moderately intelligent, it will. Mrs Penruddock is a very proud woman and lives in a very exclusive section of the city. If it should become known that she wore imitation pearls, and above all, if it should be even hinted in the public press that these were the very pearls her own husband had given her for her golden wedding present – well, I am sure you see the point, Henry.'

'Box guys ain't too bright,' he said and rubbed his stony chin. Then he lifted his right thumb and bit it thoughtfully. He looked at the windows, at the corner of the room, at the floor. He looked at me from the corners of his eyes.

'Blackmail, huh?' he said. 'Maybe. But crooks don't mix their rackets much. Still, the guy might pass the word along. There's a chance, Walter. I wouldn't care to hock my gold fillings to buy me a piece of it, but there's a chance. How much you figure to put out?'

'A hundred dollars should be ample, but I am willing to go as high as two hundred, which is the actual cost of the imitations.'

Henry shook his head and patronized the bottle. 'Nope. The guy wouldn't uncover hisself for that kind of money. Wouldn't be worth the chance he takes. He'd dump the marbles and keep his nose clean.'

'We can at least try, Henry.'

'Yeah, but where? And we're getting low on liquor. Maybe I better put my shoes on and run out, huh?'

At that very moment, as if in answer to my unspoken prayer, a soft dull thump sounded on the door of my apartment. I opened it and picked up the final edition of the evening paper. I closed the door again and carried the paper back across the room, opening it up as I went. I touched it with my right forefinger and smiled confidently at Henry Eichelberger.

'Here. I will wager you a full quart of Old Plantation that the answer will be on the crime page of this paper.'

'There ain't any crime page,' Henry chortled. 'This is Los Angeles. I'll fade you.'

I opened the paper to page three with some trepidation, for, although I had already seen the item I was looking for in an early edition of the paper while waiting in Ada Twomey's Domestic Employment Agency, I was not certain it would appear intact in the later editions. But my faith was rewarded. It had not been removed, but appeared midway of column three exactly as before. The paragraph, which was quite short, was headed: LOU GANDESI QUESTIONED IN GEM THEFTS. 'Listen to this, Henry,' I said, and began to read. 'Acting on an anonymous tip police late last night picked up Louis G. (Lou) Gandesi, proprietor of a well-known Spring Street tavern, and quizzed him intensively concerning the recent wave of dinner-party hold-ups in an exclusive western section of this city, hold-ups during which it is alleged, more than two hundred thousand dollars' worth of valuable jewels have been torn at gun's point from women guests in fashionable homes. Gandesi was released at a late hour and refused to make any statement to reporters. "I never kibitz the cops," he said modestly. Captain William Norgaard, of the General Robbery Detail, announced himself as satisfied that Gandesi had no connection with the robberies, and that the tip was merely an act of personal spite.'

I folded the paper and threw it on the bed.

'You win, bo', Henry said, and handed me the bottle. I

took a long drink and returned it to him. 'Now what? Brace this Gandesi and take him through the hoops?'

'He may be a dangerous man, Henry. Do you think we are equal to it?'

Henry snorted contemptuously. 'Yah, a Spring Street punk. Some fat slob with a phoney ruby on his mitt. Lead me to him. We'll turn the slob inside out and drain his liver. But we're just about fresh out of liquor. All we got is maybe a pint.' He examined the bottle against the light.

'We have had enough for the moment, Henry.'

'We ain't drunk, are we? I only had seven drinks since I got here, maybe nine.'

'Certainly we are not drunk, Henry, but you take very large drinks, and we have a difficult evening before us. I think we should now get shaved and dressed, and I further think that we should wear dinner clothes. I have an extra suit which will fit you admirably, as we are almost exactly the same size. It is certainly a remarkable omen that two such large men should be associated in the same enterprise. Evening clothes impress these low characters, Henry.'

'Swell,' Henry said. 'They'll think we're mugs workin' for some big shot. This Gandesi will be scared enough to swallow his necktie.'

We decided to do as I had suggested and I laid out clothes for Henry, and while he was bathing and shaving I telephoned to Ellen Macintosh.

'Oh, Walter, I am so glad you called up,' she cried. 'Have you found anything?'

'Not yet, darling,' I said. 'But we have an idea. Henry and I are just about to put it into execution.'

'Henry, Walter? Henry who?'

'Why, Henry Eichelberger, of course, darling. Have you forgotten him so soon? Henry and I are warm friends and we—'

She interrupted me coldly. 'Are you drinking, Walter?' she demanded in a very distant voice.

'Certainly not, darling. Henry is a teetotaller.'

She sniffed sharply. I could hear the sound distinctly over

the telephone. 'But didn't Henry take the pearls?' she asked, after quite a long pause.

'Henry, angel? Of course not. Henry left because he was in love with you.'

'Oh, Walter. That ape? I'm sure you're drinking terribly. I don't ever want to speak to you again. Good-bye.' And she hung the phone up very sharply so that a painful sensation made itself felt in my ear.

I sat down in a chair with a bottle of Old Plantation in my hand wondering what I had said that could be construed as offensive or indiscreet. As I was unable to think of anything, I consoled myself with the bottle until Henry came out of the bathroom looking extremely personable in one of my pleated shirts and a wing collar and black bow tie.

It was dark when we left the apartment and I, at least, was full of hope and confidence, although a little depressed by the way Ellen Macintosh had spoken to me over the telephone.

Four

Mr Gandesi's establishment was not difficult to find, inasmuch as the first taxicab driver Henry yelled at on Spring Street directed us to it. It was called the Blue Lagoon and its interior was bathed in an unpleasant blue light. Henry and I entered it steadily, since we had consumed a partly solid meal at Mandy's Caribbean Grotto before starting out to find Mr Gandesi. Henry looked almost handsome in my second-best dinner suit, with a fringed white scarf hanging over his shoulder, a lightweight black felt hat on the back of his head (which was only a little larger than mine), and a bottle of whisky in each of the side pockets of the summer overcoat he was wearing.

The bar of the Blue Lagoon was crowded, but Henry and I went on back to the small dim dining-room behind it. A man in a dirty dinner suit came up to us and Henry asked for Gandesi, and he pointed out a fat man who sat alone at a small table in the far corner of the room. We went that way.

The man sat with a small glass of red wine in front of him and slowly twisted a large green stone on his finger. He did not look up. There were no other chairs at the table, so Henry leaned on it with both elbows.

'You Gandesi?' he said.

The man did not look up even then. He moved his thick black eyebrows together and said in an absent voice: 'Si. Yes.'

'We got to talk to you in private,' Henry told him. 'Where we won't be disturbed.'

Gandesi looked up now and there was extreme boredom in his flat black almond-shaped eyes. 'So?' he asked and shrugged. 'Eet ees about what?'

'About some pearls,' Henry said. 'Forty-nine on the string, matched and pink.'

'You sell – or you buy?' Gandesi inquired and his chin began to shake up and down as if with amusement.

'Buy,' Henry said.

The man at the table crooked his finger quietly and a very large waiter appeared at his side. 'Ees dronk,' he said lifelessly. 'Put dees men out.'

The waiter took hold of Henry's shoulder. Henry reached up carelessly, and took hold of the waiter's hand and twisted it. The waiter's face in that bluish light turned some colour I could not describe, but which was not at all healthy. He put out a low moan. Henry dropped the hand and said to me: 'Put a C-note on the table.'

I took my wallet out and extracted from it one of the two hundred-dollar bills I had taken the precaution to obtain from the cashier at the Château Moraine. Gandesi stared at the bill and made a gesture to the large waiter, who went away rubbing his hand and holding it tight against his chest.

'What for?' Gandesi asked.

'Five minutes of your time alone.'

'Ees very fonny. Okay, I bite.' Gandesi took the bill and folded it neatly and put it in his vest pocket. Then he put both hands on the table and pushed himself heavily to his feet. He started to waddle away without looking at us.

Henry and I followed him among the crowded tables to the far side of the dining-room and through a door in the wainscoting and then down a narrow dim hallway. At the end of this Gandesi opened a door into a lighted room and stood holding it for us, with a grave smile on his face. I went in first.

As Henry passed in front of Gandesi into the room the latter, with surprising agility, took a small shiny black leather club from his clothes and hit Henry on the head with it very hard. Henry sprawled forward on his hands and knees. Gandesi shut the door of the room very quickly for a man of his build and leaned against it with the small club in his left hand. Now, very suddenly, in his right appeared a short but heavy black revolver.

'Ees very fonny,' he said politely, and chuckled to himself.

Exactly what happened then I did not see clearly. Henry was at one instant on his hands and knees with his back to Gandesi. In the next, or possibly even in the same instant, something swirled like a big fish in water and Gandesi grunted. I then saw that Henry's hard blond head was buried in Gandesi's stomach and that Henry's large hands held both of Gandesi's hairy wrists. Then Henry straightened his body to its full height and Gandesi was high up in the air balanced on top of Henry's head, his mouth strained wide open and his face a dark purple colour. Then Henry shook himself, as it seemed, quite lightly, and Gandesi landed on his back on the floor with a terrible thud and lay gasping. Then a key turned in the door and Henry stood with his back to it, holding both the club and the revolver in his left hand, and solicitously feeling the pockets which contained our supply of whisky. All this happened with such rapidity that I leaned against the side wall and felt a little sick at my stomach.

'A gut-buster,' Henry drawled. 'A comedian. Wait'll I loosen my belt.'

Gandesi rolled over and got to his feet very slowly and painfully and stood swaying and passing his hand up and down his face. His clothes were covered with dust.

'This here's a cosh,' Henry said, showing me the small black club. 'He hit me with it, didn't he?'

'Why, Henry, don't you know?' I inquired.

'I just wanted to be sure,' Henry said. 'You don't do that to the Eichelbergers.'

'Okay, what you boys want?' Gandesi asked abruptly, with no trace whatever of his Italian accent.

'I told you what we wanted, dough-face.'

'I don't think I know you boys,' Gandesi said and lowered his body with care into a wooden chair beside a shabby office desk. He mopped his face and neck and felt himself in various places.

'You got the wrong idea, Gandesi. A lady living in Carondelet Park lost a forty-nine bead pearl necklace a couple of days back. A box job, but a pushover. Our outfit's carrying a little insurance on those marbles. And I'll take that C-note.'

He walked over to Gandesi and Gandesi quickly reached the folded bill from his pocket and handed it to him. Henry gave me the bill and I put it back in my wallet.

'I don't think I hear about it,' Gandesi said carefully.

'You hit me with a cosh,' Henry said. 'Listen kind of hard.'

Gandesi shook his head and then winced. 'I don't back no petermen,' he said, 'nor no heist guys. You got me wrong.'

'Listen hard,' Henry said in a low voice. 'You might hear something.' He swung the small black club lightly in front of his body with two fingers of his right hand. The slightly too-small hat was still on the back of his head, although a little crumpled.

'Henry,' I said, 'you seem to be doing all the work this evening. Do you think that is quite fair?'

'Okay, work him over,' Henry said. 'These fat guys bruise something lovely.'

By this time Gandesi had become a more natural colour and was gazing at us steadily. 'Insurance guys, huh?' he inquired dubiously.

'You said it, dough-face.'

'You try Melachrino?' Gandesi asked.

'Haw,' Henry began raucously, 'a gut-buster. A—' but I interrupted him sharply.

'One moment, Henry,' I said. Then turning to Gandesi, 'Is this Melachrino a person?' I asked him.

Gandesi's eyes rounded in surprise. 'Sure – a guy. You don't know him, huh?' A look of dark suspicion was born in his sloe-black eyes, but vanished almost as soon as it appeared.

'Phone him,' Henry said, pointing to the instrument which stood on the shabby office desk.

'Phone is bad,' Gandesi objected thoughtfully.

'So is cosh poison,' Henry said.

Gandesi sighed and turned his thick body in the chair and drew the telephone towards him. He dialled a number with an inky nail and listened. After an interval he said: 'Joe? . . . Lou. Couple insurance guys tryin' to deal on a Carondelet Park job . . . Yeah . . . No, marbles . . . You ain't heard a whisper, huh? . . . Okay, Joe.'

Gandesi replaced the phone and swung around in the chair again. He studied us with sleepy eyes. 'No soap. What insurance outfit you boys work for?'

'Give him a card,' Henry said to me.

I took my wallet out once more and withdrew one of my cards from it. It was an engraved calling card and contained nothing but my name. So I used my pocket pencil to write, Chateau Moraine Apartments, Franklin near Ivar, below the name. I showed the card to Henry and then gave it to Gandesi.

Gandesi read the card and quietly bit his finger. His face brightened suddenly. 'You boys better see Jack Lawler,' he said.

Henry stared at him closely. Gandesi's eyes were now bright and unblinking and guileless.

'Who's he?' Henry asked.

'Runs the Penguin Club. Out on the Strip – Eighty-six Forty-four Sunset or some number like that. He can find out, if any guy can.'

'Thanks,' Henry said quietly. He glanced at me. 'You believe him?'

'Well, Henry,' I said, 'I don't really think he would be above telling us an untruth.'

'Haw!' Gandesi began suddenly. 'A gut-buster! A—'

'Can it!' Henry snarled. 'That's my line. Straight goods, is it, Gandesi? About this Jack Lawler?'

Gandesi nodded vigorously. 'Straight goods, absolute. Jack Lawler got a finger in everything high-class that's touched. But he ain't easy to see.'

'Don't worry none about that. Thanks, Gandesi.'

Henry tossed the black club into the corner of the room and broke open the breech of the revolver he had been holding all this time in his left hand. He ejected the shells and then bent down and slid the gun along the floor until it disappeared under the desk. He tossed the cartridges idly in his hand for a moment and then let them spill on the floor.

'So long, Gandesi,' he said coldly. 'And keep that schnozzle of yours clean, if you don't want to be looking for it under the bed.'

He opened the door then and we both went out quickly and left the Blue Lagoon without interference from any of the employees.

Five

My car was parked a short distance away down the block. We entered it and Henry leaned his arms on the wheel and stared moodily through the windshield.

'Well, what you think, Walter?' he inquired at length.

'If you ask my opinion, Henry, I think Mr Gandesi told us a cock-and-bull story merely to get rid of us. Furthermore I do not believe he thought we were insurance agents.'

'Me too, and an extra helping,' Henry said. 'I don't figure there's any such guy as this Melachrino or this Jack Lawler and this Gandesi called up some dead number and had himself a phoney chin with it. I oughta go back there and pull his arms and legs off. The hell with the fat slob.'

'We had the best idea we could think of, Henry, and we executed it to the best of our ability. I now suggest that we return to my apartment and try to think of something else.'

'And get drunk,' Henry said, starting the car and guiding it away from the kerb.

'We could perhaps have a small allowance of liquor, Henry.'

'Yah!' Henry snorted. 'A stall. I oughta go back there and wreck the joint.'

He stopped at the intersection, although no traffic signal was in operation at the time; and raised a bottle of whisky to his lips. He was in the act of drinking when a car came up behind us and collided with our car, but not very severely. Henry choked and lowered his bottle, spilling some of the liquor on his garments.

'This town's getting too crowded,' he snarled. 'A guy can't take hisself a drink without some smart monkey bumps his elbow.'

Whoever it was in the car behind us blew a horn with some insistence, inasmuch as our car had not yet moved forward. Henry wrenched the door open and got out and went back. I heard voices of considerable loudness, the louder being Henry's voice. He came back after a moment and got into the car and drove on.

'I oughta have pulled his mush off,' he said, 'but I went soft.' He drove rapidly the rest of the way to Hollywood and the Château Moraine and we went up to my apartment and sat down with large glasses in our hands.

'We got better than a quart and a half of hooch,' Henry

said, looking at the two bottles which he had placed on the table beside others which had long since been emptied. 'That oughta be good for an idea.'

'If it isn't enough, Henry, there is an abundant further supply where it came from,' I drained my glass cheerfully.

'You seem a right guy,' Henry said. 'What makes you always talk so funny?'

'I cannot seem to change my speech, Henry. My father and mother were both severe purists in the New England tradition, and the vernacular has never come naturally to my lips, even while I was in college.'

Henry made an attempt to digest this remark, but I could see that it lay somewhat heavily on his stomach.

We talked for a time concerning Gandesi and the doubtful quality of his advice, and thus passed perhaps half an hour. Then rather suddenly the white telephone on my desk began to ring. I hurried over to it, hoping that it was Ellen Macintosh and that she had recovered from her ill humour. But it proved to be a male voice and a strange one to me. It spoke crisply, with an unpleasant metallic quality of tone.

'You Walter Gage?'

'This is Mister Gage speaking.'

'Well, *Mister* Gage, I understand you're in the market for some jewellery.'

I held the phone very tightly and turned my body and made grimaces to Henry over the top of the instrument. But he was moodily pouring himself another large portion of Old Plantation.

'That is so,' I said into the telephone, trying to keep my voice steady, although my excitement was almost too much for me. 'If by jewellery you mean pearls.'

'Forty-nine in a rope, brother. And five grand is the price.'

'Why that is entirely absurd,' I gasped. 'Five thousand dollars for those—'

The voice broke in on me rudely. 'You heard me, brother. Five grand. Just hold up the hand and count the fingers. No more, no less. Think it over. I'll call you later.'

The phone clicked dryly and I replaced the instrument shakily in its cradle. I was trembling. I walked back to my chair and sat down and wiped my face with my handkerchief.

'Henry,' I said in a low tense voice, 'it worked. But how strangely.'

Henry put his empty glass down on the floor. It was the first time that I had ever seen him put an empty glass down and leave it empty. He stared at me closely with his tight unblinking green eyes.

'Yeah?' he said gently. 'What worked, kid?' He licked his lips slowly with the tip of his tongue.

'What we accomplished down at Gandesi's place, Henry. A man just called me on the telephone and asked me if I was in the market for pearls.'

'Geez.' Henry pursed his lips and whistled gently. 'That damn dago had something after all.'

'But the price is five thousand dollars, Henry. That seems beyond reasonable explanation.'

'Huh?' Henry's eyes seemed to bulge as if they were about to depart from their orbits. 'Five grand for them ringers? The guy's nuts. They cost two C's, you said. Bugs completely is what the guy is. Five grand? Why, for five grand I could buy me enough phoney beads to cover an elephant's caboose.'

I could see that Henry seemed puzzled. He refilled our glasses silently and we stared at each other over them. 'Well, what the heck can you do with that, Walter?' he asked after a long silence.'

'Henry,' I said firmly, 'there is only one thing to do. It is true that Ellen Macintosh spoke to me in confidence, and as she did not have Mrs Penruddock's express permission to tell me about the pearls, I suppose I should respect that confidence. But Ellen is now angry with me and does not wish to speak to me, for the reason that I am drinking whisky in considerable quantities, although my speech and brain are still reasonably clear. This last is a very strange development and I think, in spite of everything, some close friend of the family should be consulted. Preferably of course, a man, someone of large business experience, and in addition to that a man who understands about jewels. There *is* such a man, Henry, and tomorrow morning I shall call upon him.'

'Geez,' Henry said. 'You coulda said all that in nine words, bo. Who is this guy?'

'His name is Mr Lansing Gallemore, and he is president of the Gallemore Jewellery Company on Seventh Street. He is a very old friend of Mrs Penruddock – Ellen has often mentioned him – and is, in fact, the very man who procured for her the imitation pearls.'

'But this guy will tip the bulls,' Henry objected.

'I do not think so, Henry. I do not think he will do anything to embarrass Mrs Penruddock in any way.'

Henry shrugged. 'Phonies are phonies,' he said. 'You can't make nothing else outa them. Not even no president of no jewellery store can't.'

'Nevertheless, there must be a reason why so large a sum is demanded, Henry. The only reason that occurs to me is blackmail and, frankly, that is a little too much for me to handle alone, because I do not know enough about the background of the Penruddock family.'

'Oke,' Henry said, sighing. 'If that's your hunch, you better follow it, Walter. And I better breeze on home and flop so as to be in good shape for the rough work, if any.'

'You would not care to pass the night here, Henry?'

'Thanks, pal, but I'm okay back at the hotel. I'll just take this spare bottle of the tiger sweat to put me to sleep. I might happen to get a call from the agency in the a.m. and would have to brush my teeth and go after it. And I guess I better change my duds back to where I can mix with the common people.'

So saying he went into the bathroom and in a short time emerged wearing his own blue serge suit. I urged him to take my car, but he said it would not be safe in his neighbourhood. He did, however, consent to use the topcoat he had been wearing and, placing in it carefully the unopened quart of whisky, he shook me warmly by the hand.

'One moment, Henry,' I said and took out my wallet. I extended a twenty-dollar bill to him.

'What's that in favour of?' he growled.

'You are temporarily out of employment, Henry, and you have done a noble piece of work this evening, puzzling as are the results. You should be rewarded and I can well afford this small token.'

'Well, thanks, pal,' Henry said. 'But it's just a loan.' His voice was gruff with emotion. 'Should I give you a buzz in the a.m.?'

'By all means. And there is one thing more that has occurred to me. Would it not be advisable for you to change your hotel? Suppose, through no fault of mine, the police learn of this theft. Would they not at least suspect you?'

'Hell, they'd bounce me up and down for hours,' Henry said. 'But what'll it get them? I ain't no ripe peach.'

'It is for you to decide, of course, Henry.'

'Yeah. Good night, pal, and don't have no nightmares.'

He left me then and I felt suddenly very depressed and lonely. Henry's company had been very stimulating to me, in spite of his rough way of talking. He was very much of a man. I poured myself a rather large drink of whisky from the remaining bottle and drank it quickly but gloomily.

The effect was such that I had an overmastering desire to speak to Ellen Macintosh at all costs. I went to the telephone and called her number. After a long wait a sleepy maid answered. But Ellen, upon hearing my name, refused to come to the telephone. That depressed me still further and I finished the rest of the whisky almost without noticing what I was doing. I then lay down on the bed and fell into fitful slumber.

Six

The busy ringing of the telephone awoke me and I saw that the morning sunlight was streaming into the room. It was nine o'clock and all the lamps were still burning. I arose feeling a little stiff and dissipated, for I was still wearing my dinner suit. But I am a healthy man with very steady nerves and I did not feel as bad as I expected. I went to the telephone and answered it.

Henry's voice said: 'How you feel, pal? I got a hangover like twelve Swedes.'

'Not too bad, Henry.'

'I got a call from the agency about a job. I better go down and take a gander at it. Should I drop around later?'

'Yes, Henry, by all means do that. By eleven o'clock I should be back from the errand about which I spoke to you last night.'

'Any more calls from you know?'

'Not yet, Henry.'

'Check. Abyssinia.' He hung up and I took a cold shower and shaved and dressed. I donned a quiet brown business suit and had some coffee sent up from the coffee shop downstairs. I also had the waiter remove the empty bottles from my apartment and gave him a dollar for his trouble. After drinking two cups of black coffee, I felt my own man once more and drove downtown to the Gallemore Jewellery Company's large and brilliant store on West Seventh Street.

It was another bright, golden morning and it seemed that somehow things should adjust themselves on so pleasant a day.

Mr Lansing Gallemore proved to be a little difficult to see, so that I was compelled to tell his secretary that it was a matter concerning Mrs Penruddock and of a confidential nature. Upon this message being carried in to him I was at once ushered into a long panelled office, at the far end of which Mr Gallemore stood behind a massive desk. He extended a thin, pink hand to me.

'Mr Gage?' I don't believe we have met, have we?'

'No, Mr Gallemore, I do not believe we have. I am the fiancé – or was until last night – of Miss Ellen Macintosh, who, as you probably know, is Mrs Penruddock's nurse. I am come to you upon a very delicate matter and it is necessary that I ask for your confidence before I speak.'

He was a man of perhaps seventy-five years of age, and very thin and tall and correct and well preserved. He had cold blue eyes but a warming smile. He was attired youthfully enough in a grey flannel suit with a red carnation at his lapel.

'That is something I make it a rule never to promise, Mr Gage,' he said. 'I think it is almost always a very unfair request. But if you assure me the matter concerns Mrs Penruddock, and is really of a delicate and confidential nature, I will make an exception.'

'It is indeed, Mr Gallemore,' I said, and thereupon told him the entire story, concealing nothing, not even the fact that I had consumed far too much whisky the day before.

He stared at me curiously at the end of my story. His finely shaped hand picked up an old-fashioned white quill pen and he slowly tickled his right ear with the feather of it.

'Mr Gage,' he said, 'can't you guess why they ask five thousand dollars for that string of pearls?'

'If you permit me to guess, in a matter of so personal a nature, I could perhaps hazard an explanation, Mr Gallemore.'

He moved the white feather around to his left ear and nodded. 'Go ahead, son.'

'The pearls are in fact real, Mr Gallemore. You are a very old friend of Mrs Penruddock – perhaps even a childhood sweetheart. When she gave you her pearls, her golden wedding present, to sell because she was in sore need of money for a generous purpose, you did not sell them, Mr Gallemore. You only pretended to sell them. You gave her twenty thousand dollars of your own money, and you returned the real pearls to her, pretending that they were an imitation made in Czechoslovakia.'

'Son, you think a lot smarter than you talk,' Mr Gallemore said. He arose and walked to a window, pulled aside a fine net curtain and looked down on the bustle of Seventh Street. He came back to his desk and seated himself and smiled a little wistfully.

'You are almost embarrassingly correct, Mr Gage,' he said, and sighed. 'Mrs Penruddock is a very proud woman, or I should simply have offered her the twenty thousand dollars as an unsecured loan. I happened to be the co-administrator of Mr Penruddock's estate and I knew that in the condition of the financial market at that time it would be out of the question to raise enough cash, without damaging the corpus of the estate beyond reason, to care for all those relatives and pensioners. So Mrs Penruddock sold her pearls – as she thought – but she insisted that no one should know about it. And I did what you have guessed. It was unimportant. I could afford the gesture. I have never married, Gage, and I am rated a wealthy man. As a matter of fact, at that time, the pearls would not have fetched more than half of what I gave her, or of what they should bring today.'

I lowered my eyes for fear this kindly old gentleman might be troubled by my direct gaze.

'So I think we had better raise that five thousand, son,' Mr Gallemore at once added in a brisk voice. 'The price is pretty low, although stolen pearls are a great deal more difficult to deal in than cut stones. If I should care to trust you that far on your face, do you think you could handle the assignment?'

'Mr Gallemore,' I said firmly but quietly, 'I am a total stranger to you and I am only flesh and blood. But I promise you by the memories of my dead and revered parents that there will be no cowardice.'

'Well, there is a good deal of the flesh and blood, son,' Mr Gallemore said kindly. 'And I am not afraid of your stealing the money, because possibly I know a little more about Miss Ellen Macintosh and her boy friend than you might suspect. Furthermore, the pearls are insured, in my name, of course, and the insurance company should really handle this affair.

But you and your funny friend seem to have got along very nicely so far, and I believe in playing out a hand. This Henry must be quite a man.'

'I have grown very attached to him, in spite of his uncouth way,' I said.

Mr Gallemore played with his white quill pen a little longer and then he brought out a large cheque book and wrote a cheque, which he carefully blotted and passed across the desk.

'If you get the pearls, I'll see that the insurance people refund this to me,' he said. 'If they like my business, there will be no difficulty about that. The bank is down at the corner and I will be waiting for their call. They won't cash the cheque without telephoning me, probably. Be careful, son, and don't get hurt.'

He shook hands with me once more and I hesitated. 'Mr Gallemore, you are placing a greater trust in me than any man ever has,' I said. 'With the exception, of course, of my own father.'

'I am acting like a damn fool,' he said with a peculiar smile. 'It is so long since I heard anyone talk the way Jane Austen writes that it is making a sucker out of me.'

'Thank you, sir. I know my language is a bit stilted. Dare I ask you to do me a small favour, sir?'

'What is it, Gage?'

'To telephone Miss Ellen Macintosh, from whom I am now a little estranged, and tell her that I am not drinking today, and that you have entrusted me with a very delicate mission.'

He laughed aloud. 'I'll be glad to, Walter. And as I know she can be trusted, I'll give her an idea of what's going on.'

I left him then and went down to the bank with the cheque, and the teller, after looking at me suspiciously, then absenting himself from his cage for a long time, finally counted out the money in hundred-dollar bills with the reluctance one might have expected, if it had been his own money.

I placed the flat packet of bills in my pocket and said: 'Now give me a roll of quarters, please.'

'A roll of quarters, sir?' His eyebrows lifted.

'Exactly. I use them for tips. And naturally I should prefer to carry them home in the wrappings.'

'Oh, I see. Ten dollars, please.'

I took the fat hard roll of coins and dropped it into my pocket and drove back to Hollywood.

Henry was waiting for me in the lobby of the Château Moraine, twirling his hat between his rough hard hands. His face looked a little more deeply lined than it had the day before and I noticed that his breath smelled of whisky. We went up to my apartment and he turned to me eagerly.

'Any luck, pal?'

'Henry,' I said, 'before we proceed further into this day I wish it clearly understood that I am not drinking. I see that already you have been at the bottle.'

'Just a pick-up, Walter,' he said a little contritely. 'That job I went out for was gone before I got there. What's the good word?'

I sat down and lit a cigarette and stared at him evenly. 'Well, Henry, I don't really know whether I should tell you or not. But it seems a little petty not to do so after all you did last night to Gandesi.' I hesitated a moment longer while Henry stared at me and pinched the muscles of his left arm. 'The pearls are real, Henry. And I have instructions to proceed with the business and I have five thousand dollars in cash in my pocket at this moment.'

I told him briefly what had happened.

He was more amazed than words could tell. 'Cripes!' he exclaimed, his mouth hanging wide open. 'You mean you got the five grand from this Gallemore – just like that?'

'Precisely that, Henry.'

'Kid,' he said earnestly, 'you got something with that daisy pan and that fluff talk that a lot of guys would give important dough to cop. Five grand – out of a business guy – just like that. Why, I'll be a monkey's uncle. I'll be a snake's daddy. I'll be a mickey finn at a woman's-club lunch.'

At that exact moment, as if my entrance to the building

had been observed, the telephone rang again and I sprang to answer it.

It was one of the voices I was awaiting, but not the one I wanted to hear with the greater longing. 'How's it looking to you this morning, Gage?'

'It is looking better,' I said. 'If I can have any assurance of honourable treatment, I am prepared to go through with it.'

'You mean you got the dough?'

'In my pocket at this exact moment.'

The voice seemed to exhale a slow breath. 'You'll get your marbles okay – if we get the price, Gage. We're in this business for a long time and we don't welsh. If we did, it would soon get around and nobody would play with us any more.'

'Yes, I can readily understand that,' I said. 'Proceed with your instructions,' I added coldly.

'Listen close, Gage. Tonight at eight sharp you be in Pacific Palisades. Know where that is?'

'Certainly. It is a small residential section west of the polo fields on Sunset Boulevard.'

'Right. Sunset goes slap through it. There's one drugstore there – open till nine. Be there waiting a call at eight sharp tonight. Alone. And I mean alone, Gage. No cops and no strong-arm guys. It's rough country down there and we got a way to get you to where we want you and know if you're alone. Get all this?'

'I am not entirely an idiot,' I retorted.

'No dummy packages, Gage. The dough will be checked. No guns. You'll be searched and there's enough of us to cover you from all angles. We know your car. No funny business, no smart work, no slip-up and nobody hurt. That's the way we do business. How's the dough fixed?'

'One-hundred-dollar bills,' I said. 'And only a few of them are new.'

'Attaboy. Eight o'clock then. Be smart, Gage.'

The phone clicked in my ear and I hung up. It rang again almost instantly. This time it was the *one* voice.

'Oh, Walter,' Ellen cried, 'I was so mean to you! Please forgive me, Walter. Mr Gallemore has told me everything and I'm so frightened.'

'There is nothing of which to be frightened,' I told her warmly. 'Does Mrs Penruddock know, darling?'

'No, darling. Mr Gallemore told me not to tell her. I am phoning from a store down on Sixth Street. Oh, Walter, I really am frightened. Will Henry go with you?'

'I am afraid not, darling. The arrangements are all made and they will not permit it. I must go alone.'

'Oh, Walter! I'm terrified. I can't bear the suspense.'

'There is nothing to fear,' I assured her. 'It is a simple business transaction. And I am not exactly a midget.'

'But, Walter – oh, I *will* try to be brave, Walter. Will you promise me just one teensy-weensy little thing?'

'Not a drop, darling,' I said firmly. 'Not a single solitary drop.'

'Oh, Walter!'

There was a little more of that sort of thing, very pleasant to me in the circumstances, although possibly not of great interest to others. We finally parted with my promise to telephone as soon as the meeting between the crooks and myself had been consummated.

I turned from the telephone to find Henry drinking deeply from a bottle he had taken from his hip pocket.

'Henry!' I cried sharply.

He looked at me over the bottle with a shaggy determined look. 'Listen, pal,' he said in a low hard voice. 'I got enough of your end of the talk to figure the set-up. Some place out in the tall weeds and you go alone and they feed you the old cosh poison and take your dough and leave you lying – with the marbles still in their kitty. Nothing doing, pal. I said – nothing doing!' He almost shouted the last words.

'Henry, it is my duty and I must do it,' I said quietly.

'Haw!' Henry snorted. 'I say no. You're a nut, but you're a sweet guy on the side. I say no. Henry Eichelberger of the Wisconsin Eichelbergers – in fact, I might just as leave say of the Milwaukee Eichelbergers – says no. And he says it with both hands working.' He drank again from his bottle.

'You certainly will not help matters by becoming intoxicated,' I told him rather bitterly.

He lowered the bottle and looked at me with amazement written all over his rugged features. 'Drunk, Walter?' he boomed. 'Did I hear you say drunk? An Eichelberger drunk? Listen, son. We ain't got a lot of time now. It would take maybe three months. Some day when you got three months and maybe five thousand gallons of whisky and a funnel, I would be glad to take my own time and show you what an Eichelberger looks like when drunk. You wouldn't believe it. Son, there wouldn't be nothing left of this town but a few sprung girders and a lot of busted bricks, in the middle of which – Geez, I'll get talking English myself if I hang around you much longer – in the middle of which, peaceful, with no human life nearer than maybe fifty miles, Henry Eichelberger will be on his back smiling at the sun. Drunk, Walter. Not stinking drunk, not even country-club drunk. But you could use the word drunk and I wouldn't take no offence.'

He sat down and drank again. I stared moodily at the floor. There was nothing for me to say.

'But that,' Henry said, 'is some other time. Right now I am just taking my medicine. I ain't myself without a slight touch of delirium tremens, as the guy says. I was brought up on it. And I'm going with you, Walter. Where is this place at?'

'It's down near the beach, Henry, and you are not going with me. If you must get drunk – get drunk, but you are not going with me.'

'You got a big car, Walter. I'll hide in back on the floor under a rug. It's a cinch.'

'No, Henry.'

'Walter, you are a sweet guy,' Henry said, 'and I am going with you into this frame. Have a smell from the barrel, Walter. You look to me kind of frail.'

We argued for an hour and my head ached and I began to feel very nervous and tired. It was then that I made what might have been a fatal mistake. I succumbed to Henry's blandishments and took a small portion of whisky, purely for medicinal purposes. This made me feel so much more relaxed that I took another and larger portion. I had had no food except coffee that morning and only a very light dinner the evening before. At the end of another hour Henry had been out for two more bottles of whisky and I was as bright as a bird. All difficulties had now disappeared and I had agreed heartily that Henry should lie in the back of my car hidden by a rug and accompany me to the rendezvous.

We had passed the time very pleasantly until two o'clock, at which hour I began to feel sleepy and lay down on the bed, and fell into a deep slumber.

Seven

When I awoke again it was almost dark. I rose from the bed with panic in my heart, and also a sharp shoot of pain through my temples. It was only six-thirty, however. I was alone in the apartment and lengthening shadows were stealing across the floor. The display of empty whisky bottles on the table was very disgusting. Henry Eichelberger was nowhere to be seen. With an instinctive pang, of which I was almost immediately ashamed, I hurried to my jacket hanging on the back of a chair and plunged my hand into the inner breast pocket. The packet of bills was there intact. After a brief hesitation, and with a feeling of secret guilt, I drew them out and slowly counted them over. Not a bill was missing. I replaced the money and tried to smile at myself for this lack of trust, and then switched on a light and went into the bathroom to take alternate hot and cold showers until my brain was once more comparatively clear.

I had done this and was dressing in fresh linen when a key turned in the lock and Henry Eichelberger entered with two wrapped bottles under his arm. He looked at me with what I thought was genuine affection.

'A guy that can sleep it off like you is a real champ, Walter,' he said admiringly. 'I snuck your keys so as not to wake you. I had to get some eats and some more hooch. I done a little solo drinking, which as I told you is against my principles, but this is a big day. However, we take it easy from now on as to the hooch. We can't afford no jitters till it's all over.'

He had unwrapped a bottle while he was speaking and poured me a small drink. I drank it gratefully and immediately felt a warm glow in my veins.

'I bet you looked in your poke for that deck of mazuma,' Henry said, grinning at me.

I felt myself reddening, but I said nothing. 'Okay, pal, you done right. What the heck do you know about Henry Eichelberger anyways? I done something else.' He reached behind him and drew a short automatic from his hip pocket. 'If these boys wanta play rough,' he said, 'I got me five bucks worth of iron that don't mind playin' rough a little itself. And the Eichelbergers ain't missed a whole lot of the guys they shot at.'

'I don't like that, Henry,' I said severely. 'That is contrary to the agreement.'

'Nuts to the agreement,' Henry said. 'The boys get their dough and no cops. I'm out to see that they hand over them marbles and don't pull any fast footwork.'

I saw there was no use arguing with him, so I completed my dressing and prepared to leave the apartment. We each took one more drink and then Henry put a full bottle in his pocket and we left.

On the way down the hall to the elevator he explained in a low voice: 'I got a hack out front to tail you, just in case these boys got the same idea. You might circle a few quiet blocks so as I can find out. More like they don't pick you up till down close to the beach.'

'All this must be costing you a great deal of money, Henry,'

I told him, and while we were waiting for the elevator to come up I took another twenty-dollar bill from my wallet and offered it to him. He took the money reluctantly, but finally folded it and placed it in his pocket.

I did as Henry had suggested, driving up and down a number of the hilly streets north of Hollywood Boulevard, and presently I heard the unmistakable hoot of a taxicab horn behind me. I pulled over to the side of the road. Henry got out of the cab and paid off the driver and got into my car beside me.

'All clear,' he said. 'No tail. I'll just keep kind of slumped down and you better stop somewhere for some groceries on account of if we have to get rough with these mugs, a full head of steam will help.'

So I drove westward and dropped down to Sunset Boulevard and presently stopped at a crowded drive-in restaurant where we sat at the counter and ate a light meal of omelette and black coffee. We then proceeded on our way. When we reached Beverly Hills, Henry again made me wind in and out through a number of residential streets where he observed very carefully through the rear window of the car.

Fully satisfied at last we drove back to Sunset, and without incident onwards through Bel-Air and the fringes of Westwood, almost as far as the Riviera polo field. At this point, down in the hollow, there is a canyon called Mandeville Canyon, a very quiet place. Henry had me drive up this for a short distance. We then stopped and had a little whisky from his bottle and he climbed into the back of the car and curled his big body up on the floor, with the rug over him and his automatic pistol and his bottle down on the floor conveniently to his hand. That done I once more resumed my journey.

Pacific Palisades is a district whose inhabitants seem to retire rather early. When I reached what might be called the business centre nothing was open but the drugstore beside the bank. I parked the car, with Henry remaining silent under the rug in the back, except for a slight gurgling noise I noticed as I stood on the dark sidewalk. Then I went into the drugstore and saw by its clock that it was now fifteen minutes to eight. I bought a package of cigarettes and lit one and took up my position near the open telephone booth.

The druggist, a heavy-set red-faced man of uncertain age, had a small radio up very loud and was listening to some foolish serial. I asked him to turn it down, as I was expecting an important telephone call. This he did, but not with any good grace, and immediately retired to the back part of his store whence I saw him looking out at me malignantly through a small glass window.

At precisely one minute to eight by the drugstore clock the phone rang sharply in the booth. I hastened into it and pulled the door tight shut. I lifted the receiver, trembling a little in spite of myself.

It was the same cool metallic voice. 'Gage?'

'This is Mr Gage.'

'You done just what I told you?'

'Yes,' I said. 'I have the money in my pocket and I am entirely alone.' I did not like the feeling of lying so brazenly, even to a thief, but I steeled myself to it.

'Listen, then. Go back about three hundred feet the way you come. Beside the firehouse there's a service station, closed up, painted green and red and white. Beside that, going south, is a dirt road. Follow it three-quarters of a mile and you come to a white fence of four-by-four built almost across the road. You can just squeeze your car by at the left side. Dim your lights and get through there and keep going down the little hill into a hollow with sage all around. Park there, cut your lights, and wait. Get it?'

'Perfectly,' I said coldly, 'and it shall be done exactly that way.'

'And listen, pal. There ain't a house in half a mile, and there ain't any folks around at all. You got ten minutes to get there. You're watched right this minute. You get there fast and you get there alone – or you got a trip for biscuits. And don't light no matches or pills nor use no flashlights. On your way.'

The phone went dead and I left the booth. I was scarcely outside the drugstore before the druggist rushed at his radio and turned it up to a booming blare. I got into my car and turned it and drove back along Sunset Boulevard, as directed. Henry was as still as the grave on the floor behind me.

I was now very nervous and Henry had all the liquor which we had brought with us. I reached the firehouse in no time at all and through its front window I could see four firemen playing cards. I turned to the right down the dirt road past the red-and-green-and-white service station and almost at once the night was so still, in spite of the quiet sound of my car, that I could hear the crickets and treefrogs chirping and trilling in all directions, and from some nearby watery spot came the hoarse croak of a solitary bullfrog.

The road dipped and rose again and far off there was a yellow window. Then ahead of me, ghostly in the blackness of the moon-less night, appeared the dim white barrier across the road. I noted the gap at the side and then dimmed my headlamps and steered carefully through it and so on down a rough short hill into an oval-shaped hollow space surrounded by low brush and plentifully littered with empty bottles and cans and pieces of paper. It was entirely deserted, however, at this dark hour. I stopped my car and shut off the ignition, and the lights, and sat there motionless, hands on the wheel.

Behind me I heard no murmur of sound from Henry. I waited possibly five minutes, although it seemed much longer, but nothing happened. It was very still, very lonely, and I did not feel happy.

Finally there was a faint sound of movement behind me and I looked back to see the pale blur of Henry's face peering at me from under the rug.

His voice whispered huskily: 'Anything stirring, Walter?'

I shook my head at him vigorously and he once more pulled the rug over his face. I heard a faint sound of gurgling.

Fully fifteen minutes passed before I dared to move again. By this time the tension of waiting had made me stiff. I therefore boldly unlatched the door of the car and stepped out upon the rough ground. Nothing happened. I walked slowly back and forth with my hands in my pockets. More and more time dragged by. More than half an hour had now elapsed and I became impatient. I went to the rear window of the car and spoke softly into the interior.

'Henry, I fear we have been victimized in a very cheap way. I fear very much that this is nothing but a low practical joke on the part of Mr Gandesi in retaliation for the way you handled him last night. There is no one here and only one possible way of arriving. It looks to me like a very unlikely place for the sort of meeting we have been expecting.'

'The son of a bitch!' Henry whispered back, and the gurgling sound was repeated in the darkness of the car. Then there was movement and he appeared free of the rug. The door opened against my body. Henry's head emerged. He looked in all directions his eyes could command. 'Sit down on the running board,' he whispered. 'I'm getting out. If they got a bead on us from them bushes, they'll only see one head.'

I did what Henry suggested and turned my collar up high and pulled my hat down over my eyes. As noiselessly as a shadow Henry stepped out of the car and shut the door without sound and stood before me ranging the limited horizon with his eyes. I could see the dim reflection on the gun in his hand. We remained thus for ten more minutes.

Henry then got angry and threw discretion to the winds. 'Suckered!' he snarled. 'You know what happened, Walter?'

'No, Henry. I do not.'

'It was just a tryout, that's what it was. Somewhere along the line these dirty so-and-so's checked on you to see you did play ball, and then again they checked on you at that drugstore back there. I bet you a pair of solid platinum bicycle wheels that was a long-distance call you caught back there.'

'Yes, Henry, now that you mention it, I am sure it was,' I said sadly.

'There you are, kid. The bums ain't even left town. They are sitting back there beside their plush-lined spittoons giving you the big razzoo. And tomorrow this guy calls you again on the phone and says Okay so far, but they had to be careful, and they will try again tonight maybe out in San Fernando Valley and the price will be upped to ten grand, on account of their extra trouble. I oughta go back there and twist that Gandesi so he would be lookin' up his left pants leg.'

'Well, Henry,' I said, 'after all, I did not do exactly what they told me to, because you insisted on coming with me. And perhaps they are more clever than you think. So I think the best thing now is to go back to town and hope there will be a chance tomorrow to try again. And you must promise me faithfully not to interfere.'

'Nuts!' Henry said angrily. 'Without me along they would take you the way the cat took the canary. You are a sweet guy, Walter, but you don't know as many answers as Baby Leroy. These guys are thieves and they have a string of marbles that might probably bring them twenty grand with careful handling. They are out for a quick touch, but they will squeeze all they can just the same. I oughta go back to that fat wop Gandesi right now. I could do things to that slob that ain't been invented yet.'

'Now, Henry, don't get violent,' I said.

'Haw,' Henry snarled. 'Them guys give me an ache in the back of my lap.' He raised his bottle to his lips with his left hand and drank thirstily. His voice came down a few tones and sounded more peaceful. 'Better dip the bill, Walter. The party's a flop.'

'Perhaps you are right, Henry,' I sighed. 'I will admit that my stomach has been trembling like an autumn leaf for all of half an hour.'

So I stood up boldly beside him and poured a liberal portion of the fiery liquid down my throat. At once my courage revived. I handed the bottle back to Henry and he placed it carefully down on the running board. He stood beside me dancing the short automatic pistol up and down on the broad palm of his hand.

'I don't need no tools to handle that bunch. The hell with

it.' And with a sweep of his arm he hurled the pistol off among the bushes, where it fell to the ground with a muffled thud. He walked away from the car and stood with his arms akimbo, looking up at the sky.

I moved over beside him and watched his averted face, in so far as I was able to see it in that dim light. A strange melancholy came over me. In the brief time I had known Henry I had grown very fond of him.

'Well, Henry,' I said at last, 'what is the next move?'

'Beat it on home, I guess,' he said slowly and mournfully. 'And get good and drunk.' He doubled his hands into fists and shook them slowly. Then he turned to face me. 'Yeah,' he said. 'Nothing else to do. Beat it on home, kid, is all that is left to us.'

'Not quite yet, Henry,' I said softly.

I took my right hand out of my pocket. I have large hands. In my right hand nestled the roll of wrapped quarters which I had obtained at the bank that morning. My hand made a large fist around them.

'Good night, Henry,' I said quietly, and swung my fist with all the weight of my arm and body. 'You had two strikes on me, Henry,' I said. 'The big one is still left.'

But Henry was not listening to me. My fist with the wrapped weight of metal inside it had caught him fairly and squarely on the point of his jaw. His legs became boneless and he pitched straight forward, brushing my sleeve as he fell. I stepped quickly out of his way.

Henry Eichelberger lay motionless on the ground, as limp as a rubber glove.

I looked down at him a little sadly, waiting for him to stir, but he did not move a muscle. He lay inert, completely unconscious. I dropped the roll of quarters back into my pocket, bent over him, searched him thoroughly, moving him around like a sack of meal, but it was a long time before I found the pearls. They were twined around his ankle inside his left sock.

'Well, Henry,' I said, speaking to him for the last time,

although he could not hear me, 'you are a gentleman, even if you are a thief. You could have taken the money a dozen times this afternoon and given me nothing. You could have taken it a little while ago when you had the gun in your hand, but even that repelled you. You threw the gun away and we were man to man, far from help, far from interference. And even then you hesitated, Henry. In fact, Henry, I think for a successful thief you hesitated just a little too long. But as a man of sporting feelings I can only think the more highly of you. Good-bye, Henry, and good luck.'

I took my wallet out and withdrew a one-hundred-dollar bill and placed it carefully in the pocket where I had seen Henry put his money. Then I went back to the car and took a drink out of the whisky bottle and corked it firmly and laid it beside him, convenient to his right hand.

I felt sure that when he awakened he would need it.

Eight

It was past ten o'clock when I returned home to my apartment, but I at once went to the telephone and called Ellen Macintosh. 'Darling!' I cried. 'I have the pearls.'

I caught the sound of her indrawn breath over the wire. 'Oh, darling,' she said tensely and excitedly, 'and you are not hurt? They did not hurt you, darling? They just took the money and let you go?'

'There were no "they" darling,' I said proudly. 'I still have Mr Gallemore's money intact. There was only Henry.'

'Henry!' she cried in a very strange voice. 'But I thought—Come over here at once, Walter Gage, and tell me—'

'I have whisky on my breath, Ellen.'

'Darling! I'm sure you needed it. Come at once.'

So once more I went down to the street and hurried to Carondelet Park and in no time at all was at the Penruddock residence. Ellen came out on the porch to meet me and we talked there quietly in the dark, holding hands, for the household had gone to bed. As simply as I could I told her my story.

'But, darling,' she said at last, 'how did you know it was Henry? I thought Henry was your friend. And this other voice on the telephone—'

'Henry *was* my friend,' I said a little sadly, 'and that is what destroyed him. As to the voice on the telephone, that was a small matter and easily arranged. Henry was away from me a number of times to arrange it. There was just one small point that gave me thought. After I gave Gandesi my private card with the name of my apartment house scribbled upon it, it was necessary for Henry to communicate to his confederate that we had seen Gandesi and given him my name and address. For of course when I had this foolish, or perhaps not so very foolish idea of visiting some well-known underworld character in order to send a message that we would buy back the pearls, this was Henry's opportunity to make me think the telephone message came as a result of our talking to Gandesi, and telling him our difficulty. But since the first call came to me at my apartment before Henry had had a chance to inform his confederate of our meeting with Gandesi, it was obvious that a trick had been employed.

'Then I recalled that a car had bumped into us from behind and Henry had gone back to abuse the driver. And of course the bumping was deliberate, and Henry had made the opportunity for it on purpose, and his confederate was in the car. So Henry, while pretending to shout at him, was able to convey the necessary information.'

'But, Walter,' Ellen said, having listened to this explanation a little impatiently, 'that is a very small matter. What I really want to know is how you decided that Henry had the pearls at all.'

'But you told me he had them,' I said. 'You were quite

sure of it. Henry is a very durable character. It would be just like him to hide the pearls somewhere, having no fear of what the police might do to him, and get another position and then after perhaps quite a long time, retrieve the pearls and quietly leave this part of the country.'

Ellen shook her head impatiently in the darkness of the porch. 'Walter,' she said sharply, 'you are hiding something. You could not have been sure and you would not have hit Henry in that brutal way, unless you had been sure. I know you well enough to know that.'

'Well, darling,' I said modestly, 'there was indeed another small indication, one of those foolish trifles which the cleverest men overlook. As you know, I do not use the regular apartment-house telephone, not wishing to be annoyed by canvassers and such people. The phone which I use is a private line and its number is unlisted. But the calls I received from Henry's confederate came over that phone, and Henry had been in my apartment a great deal, and I had been careful not to give Mr Gandesi that number, as I was perfectly sure from the beginning that Henry had the pearls, if only I could get him to bring them out of hiding.'

'Oh, darling,' Ellen cried, and threw her arms around me. 'How brave you are, and I really think that you are actually clever in your own peculiar way. Do you believe that Henry was in love with me?'

But that was a subject in which I had no interest whatever. I left the pearls in Ellen's keeping and late as the hour now was I drove at once to the residence of Mr Lansing Gallemore and told him my story and gave him back his money.

A few months later I was happy to receive a letter postmarked in Honolulu and written on a very inferior brand of paper.

Well, pal, that Sunday punch of yours was the money and I did not think you had it in you, altho of course I was not set for it. But it was a pip and made me think of you for a week every time I brushed my teeth. It was too bad I had to scram because you are a sweet guy altho a little on the goofy side and I'd like

to be getting plastered with you right now instead of wipin oil valves where I am at which is not where this letter is mailed by several thousand miles. There is just two things I would like you to know and they are both kosher. I did fall hard for that tall blonde and this was the main reason I took my time from the old lady. Glomming the pearls was just one of those screwy ideas a guy can get when he is dizzy with a dame. It was a crime the way they left them marbles lying around in that bread box and I worked for a Frenchy once in Djibouty and got to know pearls enough to tell them from snowballs. But when it came to the clinch down there in that brush with us two alone and no holds barred I just was too soft to go through with the deal. Tell that blonde you got a loop on I was asking for her.
Ys as ever,
Henry Eichelberger (*alias*)

PS What do you know, that punk that did the phone work on you tried to take me for a fifty cut on that C-note you tucked in my vest. I had to twist the sucker plenty.
Ys H.E. (*alias*)

Finger Man

I got away from the Grand Jury a little after four, and then sneaked up the back stairs to Fenweather's office. Fenweather, the DA, was a man with severe, chiselled features and the grey temples women love. He played with a pen on his desk and said: 'I think they believed you. They might even indict Manny Tinnen for the Shannon kill this afternoon. If they do, then is the time you begin to watch your step.'

I rolled a cigarette around in my fingers and finally put it in my mouth. 'Don't put any men on me, Mr Fenweather. I know the alleys in this town pretty well, and your men couldn't stay close enough to do me any good.'

He looked towards one of the windows. 'How well do you know Frank Dorr?' he asked, with his eyes away from me.

'I know he's a big politico, a fixer you have to see if you want to open a gambling hell or a bawdy house – or if you want to sell honest merchandise to the city.'

'Right.' Fenweather spoke sharply, and brought his head around towards me. Then he lowered his voice. 'Having the goods on Tinnen was a surprise to a lot of people. If Frank Dorr had an interest in getting rid of Shannon who was the head of the Board where Dorr's supposed to get his contracts, it's close enough to make him take chances. And I'm told he and Manny Tinnen had dealings. I'd sort of keep an eye on him, if I were you.'

I grinned. 'I'm just one guy,' I said. 'Frank Dorr covers a lot of territory. But I'll do what I can.'

Fenweather stood up and held his hand across the desk. He said: 'I'll be out of town for a couple of days. I'm leaving tonight, if this indictment comes through. Be careful – and if anything should happen to go wrong, see Bernie Ohls, my chief investigator.'

I said: 'Sure.'

We shook hands and I went out past a tired-looking girl who gave me a tired smile and wound one of her lax curls up on the back of her neck as she looked at me. I got back to my office soon after four-thirty. I stopped outside the door of the little reception room for a moment, looking at it. Then I opened it and went in, and, of course, there wasn't anybody there.

There was nothing there but an old red davenport, two odd chairs, a bit of carpet, and a library table with a few old magazines on it. The reception room was left open for visitors to come in and sit down and wait – if I had any visitors and they felt like waiting.

I went across and unlocked the door into my private office, lettered PHILIP MARLOWE . . . INVESTIGATIONS.

Lou Harger was sitting on a wooden chair on the side of the desk away from the window. He had bright yellow gloves clamped on the crook of a cane, a green snap-brim hat set too far back on his head. Very smooth black hair showed under the hat and grew too low on the nape of his neck.

'Hello. I've been waiting,' he said, and smiled languidly.

' 'Lo, Lou. How did you get in here?'

'The door must have been unlocked. Or maybe I had a key that fitted. Do you mind?'

I went around the desk and sat down in the swivel chair. I put my hat down on the desk, picked up a bulldog pipe out of an ash-tray and began to fill it up.

'It's all right as long as it's you,' I said. 'I just thought I had a better lock.'

He smiled with his full red lips. He was a very good-looking boy. He said: 'Are you still doing business, or will you spend the next month in an hotel room drinking liquor with a couple of Headquarters boys?'

'I'm still doing business – if there's any business for me to do.'

I lit my pipe, leaned back and stared at his clear olive skin, straight, dark eyebrows.

He put his cane on top of the desk and clasped his yellow gloves on the glass. He moved his lips in and out.

'I have a little something for you. Not a hell of a lot. But there's car fare in it.'

I waited.

'I'm making a little play at Las Olindas tonight,' he said. 'At Canales' place.'

'The white smoke?'

'Uh-huh. I think I'm going to be lucky – and I'd like to have a guy with a rod.'

I took a fresh pack of cigarettes out of a top drawer and slid them across the desk. Lou picked them up and began to break the pack open.

I said: 'What kind of a play?'

He got a cigarette halfway out and stared down at it. There was a little something in his manner I didn't like.

'I've been closed up for a month now. I wasn't makin' the kind of money it takes to stay open in this town. The Headquarters boys have been putting the pressure on since repeal. They have bad dreams when they see themselves trying to live on their pay.'

I said: 'It doesn't cost any more to operate here than anywhere else. And here you pay it all to one organization. That's something.'

Lou Harger jabbed the cigarette in his mouth. 'Yeah – Frank Dorr,' he snarled. 'That fat, blood-suckin' sonofabitch!'

I didn't say anything. I was way past the age when it's fun to swear at people you can't hurt. I watched Lou light his cigarette with my desk lighter. He went on, through a puff of smoke: 'It's a laugh, in a way. Canales bought a new wheel – from some grafters in the sheriff's office. I know Pina, Canales' head croupier pretty well. The wheel is one they took away from me. It's got bugs – and I know the bugs.'

'And Canales don't ... That sounds just like Canales,' I said.

Lou didn't look at me. 'He gets a nice crowd down there,' he said. 'He has a small dance floor and a five-piece Mexican band to help the customers relax. They dance a bit and then go back for another trimming, instead of going away disgusted.'

I said: 'What do *you* do?'

'I guess you might call it a system,' he said softly, and looked at me under his long lashes.

I looked away from him, looked around the room. It had a rust-red carpet, five green filing cases in a row under an advertising calendar, an old customer in the corner, a few walnut chairs, net curtains over the windows. The fringe of the curtains was dirty from blowing about in the draught. There was a bar of late sunlight across my desk and it showed up the dust.

'I get it like this,' I said. 'You think you have that roulette wheel tamed and you expect to win enough money so that Canales will be mad at you. You'd like to have some protection along – me. I think it's screwy.'

'It's not screwy at all,' Lou said. 'Any roulette wheel has a tendency to work in a certain rhythm. If you know the wheel very well indeed—'

I smiled and shrugged. 'Okay, I wouldn't know about that. I don't know enough roulette. It sounds to me like you're being a sucker for your own racket, but I could be wrong. And that's not the point anyway.'

'What is?' Lou asked thinly.

'I'm not much stuck on bodyguarding – but maybe that's not the point either. I take it I'm supposed to think this play is on the level. Suppose I don't, and walk out on you, and you get in a box. Or suppose I think everything is aces, but Canales don't agree with me and gets nasty.'

'That's why I need a guy with a rod,' Lou said, without moving a muscle except to speak.

I said evenly: 'If I'm tough enough for the job – and I didn't know I was – that still isn't what worries me.'

'Forget it,' Lou said. 'It breaks me up enough to know you're worried.'

I smiled a little more and watched his yellow gloves moving

around on top of the desk, moving too much. I said slowly: 'You're the last guy in the world to be getting expense money that way just now. I'm the last guy to be standing behind you while you do it. That's all.'

Lou said: 'Yeah.' He knocked some ash off his cigarette down on the glass top, bent his head to blow it off. He went on, as if it was a new subject: 'Miss Glenn is going with me. She's a tall red-head, a swell looker. She used to model. She's nice people in any kind of a spot and she'll keep Canales from breathing on my neck. So we'll make out. I just thought I'd tell you.'

I was silent for a minute, then I said: 'You know damn well I just got through telling the Grand Jury it was Manny Tinnen I saw lean out of that car and cut the ropes on Art Shannon's wrists after they pushed him on to the roadway, filled with lead.'

Lou smiled faintly at me. 'That'll make it easier for the grafters on the big time; the fellows who take the contracts and don't appear in the business. They say Shannon was square and kept the Board in line. It was a nasty bump-off.'

I shook my head. I didn't want to talk about that. I said: 'Canales has a noseful of junk a lot of the time. And maybe he doesn't go for redheads.'

Lou stood up slowly and lifted his cane off the desk. He stared at the tip of one yellow finger. He had an almost sleepy expression. Then he moved towards the door, swinging his cane.

'Well, I'll be seein' you some time,' he drawled.

I let him get his hand on the knob before I said: 'Don't go away sore, Lou. I'll drop down to Las Olindas, if you have to have me. But I don't want any money for it, and for Pete's sake don't pay any more attention to me than you have to.'

He licked his lips softly and didn't quite look at me. 'Thanks, keed. I'll be as careful as hell.'

He went out then and his yellow glove disappeared around the edge of the door.

I sat still for about five minutes and then my pipe got too

hot. I put it down, looked at my strap watch, and got up to switch on a small radio in the corner beyond the end of the desk. When the AC hum died down the last tinkle of a chime came out of the horn, then a voice was saying:

'KLI now brings you its regular early evening broadcast of local news releases. An event of importance this afternoon was the indictment returned late today against Maynard J. Tinnen by the Grand Jury. Tinnen is a well-known City Hall lobbyist and man about town. The indictment, a shock to his many friends, was based almost entirely on the testimony—'

My telephone rang sharply and a girl's cool voice said in my ear: 'One moment, please. Mr Fenweather is calling you.'

He came on at once. 'Indictment returned. Take care of the boy.'

I said I was just getting it over the radio. We talked a short moment and then he hung up, after saying he had to leave at once to catch a plane.

I leaned back in my chair again and listened to the radio without exactly hearing it. I was thinking what a damn fool Lou Harger was and that there wasn't anything I could do to change that.

Two

It was a good crowd for a Tuesday but nobody was dancing. Around ten o'clock the little five-piece band got tired of messing around with a rumba that nobody was paying any attention to. The marimba player dropped his sticks and reached under his chair for a glass. The rest of the boys lit cigarettes and just sat there looking bored.

I leaned sidewise against the bar, which was on the same side of the room as the orchestra stand. I was turning a small glass of tequila around on the top of the bar. All the business was at the centre one of the three roulette tables.

The bartender leaned beside me, on his side of the bar. 'The flame-top gal must be pickin' them,' he said.

I nodded without looking at him. 'She's playing with fistfuls now,' I said. 'Not even counting it.'

The red-haired girl was tall. I could see the burnished copper of her hair between the heads of the people behind her. I could see Lou Harger's sleek head beside hers. Everybody seemed to be playing standing up.

'You don't play?' the bartender asked me.

'Not on Tuesdays. I had some trouble on a Tuesday once.'

'Yeah? Do you like that stuff straight, or would I smooth it out for you?'

'Smooth it out with what?' I said. 'You got a wood rasp handy?'

He grinned. I drank a little more of the tequila and made a face.

'Did somebody invent this stuff on purpose?'

'I wouldn't know, mister.'

'What's the limit over there?'

'I wouldn't know that either. How the boss feels, I guess.'

The roulette tables were in a row near the far wall. A low railing of gilt metal joined their ends and the players were outside the railing.

Some kind of a confused wrangle started at the centre table. Half a dozen people at the two end tables grabbed their chips up and moved across.

Then a clear, very polite voice, with a slight foreign accent, spoke out: 'If you will just be patient, madame ... Mr Canales will be here in a minute.'

I went across, squeezed near the railing. Two croupiers stood near me with their heads together and their eyes looking sidewise. One moved a rake slowly back and forth beside the idle wheel. They were staring at the red-haired girl.

She wore a high-cut black evening gown. She had fine white shoulders, was something less than beautiful and more than pretty. She was leaning on the edge of the table, in front of the wheel. Her long eyelashes were twitching. There was a big pile of money and chips in front of her.

She spoke monotonously, as if she had said the same thing several times already.

'Get busy and spin that wheel! You take it away fast enough, but you don't like to dish it out.'

The croupier in charge smiled a cold, even smile. He was tall, dark, disinterested. 'The table can't cover your bet,' he said with calm precision. 'Mr Canales, perhaps—' He shrugged neat shoulders.

The girl said: 'It's your money, highpockets. Don't you want it back?'

Lou Harger licked his lips beside her, put a hand on her arm, stared at the pile of money with hot eyes. He said gently: 'Wait for Canales . . .'

'To hell with Canales! I'm hot – and I want to stay that way.'

A door opened at the end of the tables and a very slight, very pale man came into the room. He had straight, lustreless black hair, a high bony forehead, flat, impenetrable eyes. He had a thin moustache that was trimmed in two sharp lines almost at right angles to each other. They came down below the corners of his mouth a full inch. The effect was Oriental. His skin had a thick, glistening pallor.

He slid behind the croupiers, stopped at a corner of the centre table, glanced at the red-haired girl and touched the ends of his moustache with two fingers, the nails of which had a purplish tint.

He smiled suddenly, and the instant after it was as though he has never smiled in his life. He spoke in a dull, ironic voice.

'Good evening, Miss Glenn. You must let me send somebody with you when you go home. I'd hate to see any of that money get in the wrong pockets.'

The red-haired girl looked at him, not very pleasantly.

'I'm not leaving – unless you're throwing me out.'

Canales said: 'No? What would you like to do?'

'Bet the wad – dark meat!'

The crowd noise became a deathly silence. There wasn't a whisper of any kind of sound. Harger's face slowly got ivory-white.

Canales' face was without expression. He lifted a hand, delicately, gravely, slipped a large wallet from his dinner jacket and tossed it in front of the tall croupier.

'Ten grand,' he said in a voice that was a dull rustle of sound. 'That's my limit – always.'

The tall croupier picked the wallet up, spread it, drew out two flat packets of crisp bills, riffled them, refolded the wallet and passed it along the edge of the table to Canales.

Canales did not move to take it. Nobody moved, except the croupier.

The girl said: 'Put it on the red.'

The croupier leaned across the table and very carefully stacked her money and chips. He placed her bet for her on the red diamond. He placed his hand along the curve of the wheel.

'If no one objects,' Canales said, without looking at anyone, 'this is just the two of us.'

Heads moved. Nobody spoke. The croupier spun the wheel and sent the ball skimming in the groove with a light flirt of his left wrist. Then he drew his hands back and placed them in full view on the edge of the table, on top of it.

The red-haired girl's eyes shone and her lips slowly parted.

The ball drifted along the groove, dipped past one of the bright metal diamonds, slid down the flank of the wheel and chattered along the tines beside the numbers. Movement went out of it suddenly, with a dry click. It fell next the double-zero, in red twenty-seven. The wheel was motionless.

The croupier took up his rake and slowly pushed the two packets of bills across, added them to the stake, pushed the whole thing off the field of play.

Canales put his wallet back in his breast pocket, turned and walked slowly back to the door, went through it.

I took my cramped fingers off the top of the railing, and a lot of people broke for the bar.

Three

When Lou came up I was sitting at a little tile-top table in a corner, fooling with some more of the tequila. The little orchestra was playing a thin, brittle tango and one couple was manoeuvring self-consciously on the dance floor.

Lou had a cream-coloured overcoat on, with the collar turned up around a lot of white silk scarf. He had a fine-drawn glistening expression. He had white pigskin gloves this time and he put one of them down on the table and leaned at me.

'Over twenty-two thousand,' he said softly. 'Boy, what a take!'

I said: 'Very nice money, Lou. What kind of car are you driving?'

'See anything wrong with it?'

'The play?' I shrugged, fiddled with my glass. 'I'm not wised up on roulette, Lou ... I saw plenty wrong with your broad's manners.'

'She's not a broad,' Lou said. His voice got a little worried.

'Okay. She made Canales look like a million. What kind of car?'

'Buick sedan. Nile green, with two spotlights and those little fender lights on rods.' His voice was still worried.

I said: 'Take it kind of slow through town. Give me a chance to get in the parade.'

He moved his glove and went away. The red-haired girl was not in sight anywhere. I looked down at the watch on my wrist. When I looked up again Canales was standing across the table. His eyes looked at me lifelessly above his trick moustache.

'You don't like my place,' he said.

'On the contrary.'

'You don't come here to play.' He was telling me, not asking me.

'Is it compulsory?' I asked dryly.

A very faint smile drifted across his face. He leaned a little down and said: 'I think you are a dick. A smart dick.'

'Just a shamus,' I said. 'And not so smart. Don't let my long upper lip fool you. It runs in the family.'

Canales wrapped his fingers around the top of a chair, squeezed on it. 'Don't come here again – for anything.' He spoke very softly almost dreamily. 'I don't like pigeons.'

I took the cigarette out of my mouth and looked it over before I looked at him. I said: 'I heard you insulted a while back. You took it nicely ... So we won't count this one.'

He had a queer expression for a moment. Then he turned and slid away with a little sway of the shoulders. He put his feet down flat and turned them out a good deal as he walked. His walk, like his face, was a little negroid.

I got up and went out through the big white double doors into a dim lobby, got my hat and coat and put them on. I went out through another pair of double doors on to a wide veranda with scrollwork along the edge of its roof. There was sea fog in the air and the wind-blown Monterey cypresses in front of the house dripped with it. The grounds sloped gently into the dark for a long distance. Fog hid the ocean.

I had parked the car out on the street, on the other side of the house. I drew my hat down and walked soundlessly on the damp moss that covered the driveway, rounded a corner of the porch, and stopped rigidly.

A man just in front of me was holding a gun – but he didn't see me. He was holding the gun down at his side, pressed against the material of his overcoat, and his big hand made it look quite small. The dim light that reflected from the barrel seemed to come out of the fog, to be part of the fog. He was a big man, and he stood very still, poised on the balls of his feet.

I lifted my right hand very slowly and opened the top two buttons of my coat, reached inside and drew out a long .38 with a six-inch barrel. I eased it into my overcoat pocket.

The man in front of me moved, reached his left hand up to his face. He drew on a cigarette cupped inside his hand and the glow put brief light on a heavy chin, wide, dark nostrils, and a square, aggressive nose, the nose of a fighting man.

Then he dropped the cigarette and stepped on it and a quick, light step made faint noise behind me. I was far too late turning.

Something swished and I went out like a light.

Four

When I came to I was cold and wet and had a headache a yard wide. There was a soft bruise behind my right ear that wasn't bleeding. I had been put down with a cosh.

I got up off my back and saw that I was a few yards from the driveway, between two trees that were wet with fog. There was some mud on the backs of my shoes. I had been dragged off the path, but not very far.

I went through my pockets. My gun was gone, of course, but that was all – that and the idea that this excursion was all fun.

I nosed around through the fog, didn't find anything or see anyone, gave up bothering about that, and went along the blank side of the house to a curving line of palm trees and an old type arc light that hissed and flickered over the entrance to a sort of lane where I had stuck the 1925 Marmon touring car I still used for transportation. I got into it after wiping the seat off with a towel, teased the motor alive, and choked it along to a big empty street with disused car tracks in the middle.

I went from there to De Cazens Boulevard, which was the main drag of Las Olindas and was called after the man who built Canales' place long ago. After a while there was town, buildings, dead-looking stores, a service station with a night-bell, and at last a drugstore which was still open.

A dolled-up sedan was parked in front of the drugstore and I parked behind that, got out, and saw that a hatless man was sitting at the counter, talking to a clerk in a blue smock. They seemed to have the world to themselves. I started to go in then I stopped and took another look at the dolled-up sedan.

It was a Buick and of a colour that could have been Nile green in daylight. It had two spotlights and two little egg-shaped amber lights stuck up on thin nickel rods clamped to the front fenders. The window by the driver's seat was down. I went back to the Marmon and got a flash, reached in and twisted the licence holder of the Buick around, put the light on it quickly, then off again.

It was registered to Louis N. Harger.

I got rid of the flash and went into the drugstore. There was a liquor display at one side, and the clerk in the blue smock sold me a pint of Canadian Club, which I took over to the counter and opened. There were ten seats at the counter, but I sat down on the one next to the hatless man. He began to look me over, in the mirror, very carefully.

I got a cup of black coffee two-thirds full and added plenty of the rye. I drank it down and waited for a minute, to let it warm me up. Then I looked the hatless man over.

He was about twenty-eight, a little thin on top, had a healthy red face, fairly honest eyes, dirty hands and looked as if he wasn't making much money. He wore a grey whipcord jacket with metal buttons on it, pants that didn't match.

I said carelessly, in a low voice: 'Your bus outside?'

He sat very still. His mouth got small and tight and he had trouble pulling his eyes away from mine, in the mirror.

'My brother's,' he said, after a moment.

I said: 'Care for a drink? . . . Your brother is an old friend of mine.'

He nodded slowly, gulped, moved his hand slowly, but finally got the bottle and curdled his coffee with it. He drank the whole thing down. Then I watched him dig up a crumpled pack of cigarettes, spear his mouth with one, strike a match on the counter, after missing twice on his thumbnail, and inhale with a lot of very poor nonchalance that he knew wasn't going over.

I leaned close to him and said evenly: 'This doesn't *have* to be trouble.'

He said: 'Yeah . . . Wh-what's the beef?'

The clerk sidled towards us. I asked for more coffee. When I got it I stared at the clerk until he went and stood in front of the display window with his back to me. I laced my second cup of coffee and drank some of it. I looked at the clerk's back and said: 'The guy the car belongs to doesn't have a brother.'

He held himself tightly, but turned towards me. 'You think it's a hot car?'

'No.'

'You don't think it's a hot car?'

I said: 'No. I just want the story.'

'You a dick?'

'Uh-huh – but it isn't a shake-down, if that's what worries you.'

He drew hard on his cigarette and moved his spoon around in his empty cup.

'I can lose my job over this,' he said slowly. 'But I needed a hundred bucks. I'm a hack driver.'

'I guessed that,' I said.

He looked surprised, turned his head and stared at me. 'Have another drink and let's get on with it,' I said. 'Car thieves don't park them on the main street and then sit around in drugstores.'

The clerk came back from the window and hovered near us, busying himself with rubbing a rag on the coffee urn. A heavy silence fell. The clerk put the rag down, went along to the back of the store, behind the partition, and began to whistle aggressively.

The man beside me took some more of the whisky and drank it, nodding his head wisely at me. 'Listen – I brought a fare out and was supposed to wait for him. A guy and a jane come up alongside me in the Buick and the guy offers me a hundred bucks to let him wear my cap and drive my hack into town. I'm to hang around here an hour, then take his heap to the Hotel Carillon on Towne Boulevard. My cab will be there for me. He gives me the hundred bucks.'

'What was his story?' I asked.

'He said they'd been to a gambling joint and had some luck for a change. They're afraid of hold-ups on the way in. They figure there's always spotters watchin' the play.'

I took one of his cigarettes and straightened it out in my fingers. 'It's a story I can't hurt much,' I said. 'Could I see your cards?'

He gave them to me. His name was Tom Sneyd and he was a driver for the Green Top Cab Company. I corked my pint, slipped it into my side pocket, and danced a half-dollar on the counter.

The clerk came along and made change. He was almost shaking with curiosity.

'Come on, Tom,' I said in front of him. 'Let's go get that cab. I don't think you should wait around here any longer.'

We went out, and I let the Buick lead me away from the straggling lights of Las Olindas, through a series of small beach towns with little houses built on beachlots close to the ocean, and bigger ones built on the slopes of the hills behind. A window was lit here and there. The tyres sang on the moist concrete and the little amber lights on the Buick's fenders peeped back at me from the curves.

At West Cimarron we turned inland, chugged on through Canal City, and met the San Angelo Cut. It took us almost an hour to get to 5640 Towne Boulevard, which is the number of the Hotel Carillon. It is a big, rambling slate-roofed building with a basement garage and a forecourt fountain on which they play a pale green light in the evening.

Green Top Cab No 469 was parked across the street, on the dark side. I couldn't see where anybody had been shooting into it. Tom Sneyd found his cap in the driver's compartment, climbed eagerly under the wheel.

'Does that fix me up? Can I go now?' His voice was strident with relief.

I told him it was all right with me, and gave him my card.

It was twelve minutes past one as he took the corner. I climbed into the Buick and tooled it down the ramp to the garage and left it with a coloured boy who was dusting cars in slow motion. I went around to the lobby.

The clerk was an ascetic-looking young man who was reading a volume of *California Appellate Decisions* under the switchboard light. He said Lou was not in and had not been in since eleven, when he came on duty. After a short argument about the lateness of the hour and the importance of my visit, he rang Lou's apartment, but there wasn't any answer.

I went out and sat in my Marmon for a few minutes, smoked a cigarette, imbibed a little from my pint of Canadian Club. Then I went back into the Carillon and shut myself in a pay booth. I dialled the *Telegram*, asked for the City Desk, got a man named Von Ballin.

He yelped at me when I told him who I was. 'You still walking around? That ought to be a story. I thought Manny Tinnen's friends would have had you laid away in old lavender by this time.'

I said: 'Can that and listen to this. Do you know a man named Lou Harger? He's a gambler. Had a place that was raided and closed up a month ago.'

Von Ballin said he didn't know Lou personally, but he knew who he was.

'Who around your rag would know him real well?'

He thought a moment. 'There's a lad named Jerry Cross here,' he said, 'that's supposed to be an expert on night life. What did you want to know?'

'Where would he go to celebrate,' I said. Then I told him some of the story, not too much. I left out the part where I got coshed and the part about the taxi. 'He hasn't shown at his hotel,' I ended. 'I ought to get a line on him.'

'Well, if you're a friend of his—'

'Of his – not of his crowd,' I said sharply.

Von Ballin stopped to yell at somebody to take a call, then said to me softly, close to the phone: 'Come through, boy. Come through.'

'All right. But I'm talking to you, not to your sheet. I got coshed and lost my gun outside Canales' joint. Lou and his girl switched his car for a taxi they picked up. Then they dropped out of sight. I don't like it too well. Lou wasn't drunk enough to chase around town with that much dough in his pockets. And if he was, the girl wouldn't let him. She had the practical eye.'

'I'll see what I can do,' Von Ballin said. 'But it don't sound promising. I'll give you a buzz.'

I told him I lived at the Merritt Plaza, in case he had forgotten, went out and got into the Marmon again. I drove home and put hot towels on my head for fifteen minutes, then sat around in my pyjamas and drank hot whisky and lemon and called the Carillon every once in a while. At two-thirty Von Ballin called me and said no luck. Lou hadn't been pinched, he wasn't in any of the receiving hospitals, and he hadn't shown at any of the clubs Jerry Cross could think of.

At three I called the Carillon for the last time. Then I put my light out and went to sleep.

In the morning it was the same way. I tried to trace the red-haired girl a little. There were twenty-eight people named Glenn in the phone book, and three women among them. One didn't answer the other two assured me they didn't have red hair. One offered to show me.

I shaved, showered, had breakfast, walked three blocks down the hill to the Condor Building.

Miss Gleen was sitting in my little reception room.

Five

I unlocked the other door and she went in and sat in the chair where Lou had sat the afternoon before. I opened some windows, locked the outer door of the reception room, and struck a match for the unlighted cigarette she held in her ungloved and ringless left hand.

She was dressed in a blouse and plaid skirt with a loose coat over them, and a close-fitting hat that was far enough out of style to suggest a run of bad luck. But it hid almost all of her hair. Her skin was without make-up and she looked about thirty and had the set face of exhaustion.

She held her cigarette with a hand that was almost too steady, a hand on guard. I sat down and waited for her to talk.

She stared at the wall over my head and didn't say anything. After a little while I packed my pipe and smoked for a minute. Then I got up and went across to the door that opened into the hallway and picked up a couple of letters that had been pushed through the slot.

I sat down at the desk again, looked them over, read one of them twice, as if I had been alone. While I was doing this I didn't look at her directly or speak to her, but I kept an eye on her all the same. She looked like a lady who was getting nerved for something.

Finally she moved. She opened up a big black patent-leather bag and took out a fat manila envelope, pulled a rubber band off it and sat holding the envelope between the palms of her hands, with her head tilted way back and the cigarette dribbling grey smoke from the corners of her mouth.

She said slowly: 'Lou said if I ever got caught in the rain, you were the boy to see. It's raining hard where I am.'

I stared at the manila envelope. 'Lou is a pretty good friend of mine,' I said. 'I'd do anything in reason for him. Some things not in reason – like last night. That doesn't mean Lou and I always play the same games.'

She dropped her cigarette into the glass bowl of the ashtray and left it to smoke. A dark flame burned suddenly in her eyes, then went out.

'Lou is dead.' Her voice was quite toneless.

I reached over with a pencil and stabbed at the hot end of the cigarette until it stopped smoking.

She went on: 'A couple of Canales' boys got him in my apartment – with one shot from a small gun that looked like my gun. Mine was gone when I looked for it afterwards. I spent the night there with him dead . . . I had to.'

She broke quite suddenly. Her eyes turned up in her head and her head came down and hit the desk. She lay still, with the manila envelope in front of her lax hands.

I jerked a drawer open and brought up a bottle and a glass, poured a stiff one and stepped around with it, heaved her up in her chair. I pushed the edge of the glass hard against her mouth – hard enough to hurt. She struggled and swallowed. Some of it ran down her chin, but life came back into her eyes.

I left the whisky in front of her and sat down again. The flap of the envelope had come open enough for me to see currency inside, bales of currency.

She began to talk to me in a dreamy sort of voice.

'We got all big bills from the cashier, but it makes quite a package at that. There's twenty-two thousand even in the envelope. I kept out a few odd hundreds.'

'Lou was worried. He figured it would be pretty easy for Canales to catch up with us. You might be right behind and not be able to do very much about it.'

I said: 'Canales lost the money in full view of everybody there. It was good advertising – even if it hurt.'

She went on exactly as though I had not spoken. 'Going through the town we spotted a cab driver sitting in his parked cab and Lou had a brainwave. He offered the boy a C-note to let him drive the cab into San Angelo and bring the Buick to the hotel after a while. The boy took us up and we went over on another street and made the switch. We were sorry about ditching you, but Lou said you wouldn't mind. And we might get a chance to flag you.

'Lou didn't go into his hotel. We took another cab over to my place. I live at the Hobart Arms, eight hundred block on South Minter. It's a place where you don't have to answer questions at the desk. We went up to my apartment and put the lights on and two guys with masks came around the half-wall between the living-room and the dinette. One was small and thin and the other one was a big slob with a chin that stuck out under his mask like a shelf. Lou made a wrong motion and the big one shot him just the once. The gun just made a flat crack, not very loud, and Lou fell down on the floor and never moved.'

I said: 'It might be the ones that made a sucker out of me. I haven't told you about that yet.'

She didn't seem to hear that either. Her face was white and composed, but as expressionless as plaster. 'Maybe I'd better have another finger of the hootch,' she said.

I poured us a couple of drinks, and we drank them. She went on: 'They went through us, but we didn't have the money. We had stopped at an all-night drugstore and had it weighed and mailed it at a branch post office. They went through the apartment, but of course we had just come in and hadn't had time to hide anything. The big one slammed me down with his fist, and when I woke up again they were gone and I was alone with Lou dead on the floor.'

She pointed to a mark on the angle of her jaw. There was something there, but it didn't show much. I moved around in my chair a little and said: 'They passed you on the way in. Smart boys would have looked a taxi over on that road. How did they know where to go?'

'I thought that out during the night,' Miss Glenn said. 'Canales knows where I live. He followed me home once and tried to get me to ask him up.'

'Yeah,' I said, 'but why did they go to your place and how did they get in?'

'That's not hard. There's a ledge just below the windows and a man could edge along it to the fire escape. They probably had other boys covering Lou's hotel. We thought of that chance, but we didn't think about my place being known to them.'

'Tell me the rest of it,' I said.

'The money was mailed to me,' Miss Glenn explained. 'Lou was a swell boy, but a girl has to protect herself. That's why I had to stay there last night with Lou dead on the floor. Until the mail came. Then I came over here.'

I got up and looked out of the window. A fat girl was pounding a typewriter across the court. I could hear the clack of it. I sat down again, stared at my thumb.

'Did they plant the gun?' I asked.

'Not unless it's under him. I didn't look there.'

'They let you off too easy. Maybe it wasn't Canales at all. Did Lou open his heart to you much?'

She shook her head quietly. Her eyes were slate-blue now, and thoughtful, without the blank stare.

'All right,' I said. 'Just what did you think of having me do about it all?'

She narrowed her eyes a little, then put a hand out and pushed the bulging envelope slowly across the desk.

'I'm no baby and I'm in a jam. But I'm not going to the cleaners just the same. Half of this money is mine, and I want it with a clean getaway. One-half net. If I'd called the law last night, there'd have been a way to chisel me out of it ... I think Lou would like you to have his half, if you want to play with me.'

I said: 'It's big money to flash at a private dick, Miss Glenn,' and smiled wearily. 'You're a little worse off for not calling cops last night. But there's an answer to anything they might say. I think I'd better go over there and see what's broken, if anything.'

She leaned forward quickly and said: 'Will you take care of the money? ... Dare you?'

'Sure. I'll pop downstairs and put it in a safe-deposit box. You can hold one of the keys – and we'll talk split later on. I think it would be a swell idea if Canales knew he had to see me and sweller if you hid out in a little hotel where I have a friend – at least until I nose around a bit.'

She nodded. I put my hat on and put the envelope inside my belt. I went out, telling her there was a gun in the top left-hand drawer, if she felt nervous.

When I got back she didn't seem to have moved. But she

said she had phoned Canales' place and left a message for him she thought he would understand.

We went by rather devious ways to the Lorraine, at Brant and Avenue C. Nobody shot at us going over, and as far as I could see we were not trailed.

I shook hands with Jim Dolan, the day clerk at the Lorraine, with a twenty folded in my hand. He put his hand in his pocket and said he would be glad to see that 'Miss Thompson' was not bothered.

I left. There was nothing in the noon paper about Lou Harger of the Hobart Arms.

Six

The Hobart Arms was just another apartment house, in a block lined with them. It was six stories high and had a buff front. A lot of cars were parked at both kerbs all along the block. I drove through slowly and looked things over. The neighbourhood didn't have the look of having been excited about anything in the immediate past. It was peaceful and sunny, and the parked cars had a settled look, as if they were right at home.

I circled into an alley with a high board fence on each side and a lot of flimsy garages cutting it. I parked beside one that had a FOR RENT sign and went between two garbage cans into the concrete yard of the Hobart Arms, along the side to the street. A man was putting golf clubs into the back of a coupé. In the lobby a Filipino was dragging a vacuum cleaner over the rug and a dark Jewess was writing at the switchboard.

I used the automatic elevator and prowled along an upper corridor to the last door on the left. I knocked, waited, knocked again, went in with Miss Glenn's key.

Nobody was dead on the floor.

I looked at myself in the mirror that was the back of a pull-down bed, went across and looked out of a window. There was a ledge below that had once been a coping. It ran along to the fire escape. A blind man could have walked in. I didn't notice anything like footmarks in the dust on it.

There was nothing in the dinette or kitchen except what belonged there. The bedroom had a cheerful carpet and painted grey walls. There was a lot of junk in the corner, around a waste-basket, and a broken comb on the dresser held a few strands of red hair. The closets were empty except for some gin bottles.

I went back to the living-room, looked behind the wall bed, stood around for a minute, left the apartment.

The Filipino in the lobby had made about three yards with the vacuum cleaner. I leaned on the counter beside the switchboard.

'Miss Glenn?'

The dark Jewess said: 'Five-two-four,' and made a check-mark on the laundry list.

'She's not in. Has she been in late?'

She glanced up at me. 'I haven't noticed. What is it – a bill?'

I said I was just a friend, thanked her and went away. That established the fact that there had been no excitement in Miss Glenn's apartment. I went back to the alley and the Marmon.

I hadn't believed it quite the way Miss Glenn told it anyhow.

I crossed Cordova, drove a block and stopped beside a forgotten drugstore that slept behind two giant pepper trees and a dusty, cluttered window. It had a single pay booth in the corner. An old man shuffled towards me wistfully, then went away when he saw what I wanted, lowered a pair of steel spectacles on to the end of his nose and sat down again with his newspaper.

I dropped my nickel, dialled, and a girl's voice cried: 'Telegrayam!' with a tinny drawl. I asked for Von Ballin.

When I got him and he knew who it was I could hear him clearing his throat. Then his voice came close to the phone and said very distinctly: 'I've got something for you, but it's bad. I'm sorry as all hell. Your friend Harger is in the morgue. We got a flash about ten minutes ago.'

I leaned against the wall of the booth and felt my eyes getting haggard. I said: 'What else did you get?'

'Couple of radio cops picked him up in somebody's front yard or something, in West Cimarron. He was shot through the heart. It happened last night, but for some reason they only just put out the identification.'

I said: 'West Cimarron, huh? . . . Well, that takes care of that. I'll be in to see you.'

I thanked him and hung up, stood for a moment looking out through the glass at a middle-aged grey-haired man who had come into the store and was pawing over the magazine rack.

Then I dropped another nickel and dialled the Lorraine, asked for the clerk.

I said: 'Get your girl to put me on to the redhead, will you, Jim?'

I got a cigarette out and lit it, puffed smoke at the glass of the door. The smoke flattened out against the glass and swirled about in the close air. Then the line clicked and the operator's voice said: 'Sorry, your party does not answer.'

'Give me Jim again,' I said. Then, when he answered, 'Can you take time to run up and find out why she doesn't answer the phone? Maybe she's just being cagey.'

Jim said: 'You bet. I'll shoot right up with a key.'

Sweat was coming out all over me. I put the receiver down on a little shelf and jerked the booth door open. The grey-haired man looked up quickly from the magazines, then scowled and looked at his watch. Smoke poured out of the booth. After a moment I kicked the door shut and picked up the receiver again.

Jim's voice seemed to come to me from a long way off. 'She's not here. Maybe she went for a walk.'

I said: 'Yeah – or maybe it was a ride.'

I pronged the receiver and pushed on out of the booth. The grey-haired stranger slammed a magazine down so hard that it fell to the floor. He stooped to pick it up as I went past him. Then he straightened up just behind me and said quietly, but very firmly: 'Keep the hands down, and quiet. Walk on out to your heap. This is business.'

Out of the corner of my eye I could see the old man peeking short-sightedly at us. But there wasn't anything for him to see, even if he could see that far. Something prodded my back. It might have been a finger, but I didn't think it was.

We went out of the store very peacefully.

A long grey car had stopped close behind the Marmon. Its rear door was open and a man with a square face and a crooked mouth was standing with one foot out on the running board. His right hand was behind him, inside the car.

My man's voice said: 'Get in your car and drive west. Take this first corner and go about twenty-five, not more.'

The narrow street was sunny and quiet and the pepper trees whispered. Traffic threshed by on Cordova a short block away. I shrugged, opened the door of my car and got under the wheel. The grey-haired man got in very quickly beside me, watching my hands. He swung his right hand around, with a snub-nosed gun in it.

'Careful getting your keys out, buddy.'

I was careful. As I stepped on the starter a car door slammed behind, there were rapid steps, and someone got into the back seat of the Marmon. I let in the clutch and drove around the corner. In the mirror I could see the grey car making the turn behind. Then it dropped back a little.

I drove west on a street that paralleled Cordova and when we had gone a block and a half a hand came down over my shoulder from behind and took my gun away from me. The grey-haired man rested his short revolver on his leg and felt me over carefully with his free hand. He leaned back satisfied.

'Okay. Drop over to the main street and snap it up,' he said. 'But that don't mean trying to sideswipe a prowl car, if you lamp one ... Or if you think it does, try it and see.'

I made the two turns, speeded up to thirty-five and held it there We went through some nice residential districts, and then the landscape began to thin out. When it was quite thin the grey car behind dropped back, turned towards town and disappeared.

'What's the snatch for?' I asked.

The grey-haired man laughed and rubbed his broad red chin. 'Just business. The big boy wants to talk to you.'

'Canales?'

'Canales – hell! I said the *big boy*.'

I watched traffic, what there was of it that far out, and didn't speak for a few minutes. Then I said: 'Why didn't you pull it in the apartment, or in the alley?'

'Wanted to make sure you wasn't covered.'

'Who's this big boy?'

'Skip that – till we get you there. Anything else?'

'Yes. Can I smoke?'

He held the wheel while I lit up. The man in the back seat hadn't said a word at any time. After a while the grey-haired man made me pull up and move over, and he drove.

'I used to own one of these, six years ago, when I was poor,' he said jovially.

I couldn't think of a really good answer to that, so I just let smoke seep down into my lungs and wondered why, if Lou had been killed in West Cimarron, the killers didn't get the money. And if he really had been killed at Miss Glenn's apartment, why somebody had taken the trouble to carry him back to West Cimarron.

Seven

In twenty minutes we were in the foothills. We went over a hogback, drifted down a long white concrete ribbon, crossed a bridge, went halfway up the next slope and turned off on a gravel road that disappeared around a shoulder of scrub oak and manzanita. Plumes of pampas grass flared on the side of the hill, like jets of water. The wheels crunched on the gravel and skidded on the curves.

We came to a mountain cabin with a wide porch and cemented boulder foundations. The windmill of a generator turned slowly on the crest of a spur a hundred feet behind the cabin. A mountain blue jay flashed across the road, zoomed, banked sharply, and fell out of sight like a stone.

The grey-haired man tooled the car up to the porch, beside a tan-coloured Lincoln coupé, switched off the ignition and set the Marmon's long parking brake. He took the keys out, folded them carefully in their leather case, put the case away in his pocket.

The man in the back seat got out and held the door beside me open. He had a gun in his hand. I got out. The grey-haired man got out. We all went into the house.

There was a big room with walls of knotted pine, beautifully polished. We went across it walking on Indian rugs and the grey-haired man knocked carefully on a door.

A voice shouted: 'What is it?'

The grey-haired man put his face against the door and said: 'Beasley – and the guy you wanted to talk to.'

The voice inside said to come on in. Beasley opened the door, pushed me through it and shut it behind me.

It was another big room with knotted pine walls and Indian rugs on the floor. A driftwood fire hissed and puffed on a stone hearth.

The man who sat behind a flat desk was Frank Dorr, the politico.

He was the kind of man who lived to have a desk in front of him, and shove his fat stomach against it, and fiddle with things on it, and look very wise. He had a fat, muddy face, a thin fringe of white hair stuck up a little, small sharp eyes, small and very delicate hands.

What I could see of him was dressed in a slovenly grey suit, and there was a large black Persian cat on the desk in front of him. He was scratching the cat's head with one of his little neat hands and the cat was leaning against his hand. Its bushy tail flowed over the edge of the desk and fell straight down.

He said: 'Sit down,' without looking away from the cat.

I sat down in a leather chair with a very low seat. Dorr said: 'How do you like it up here? Kind of nice, ain't it? This is Toby, my girl friend. Only girl friend I got. Ain't you, Toby?'

I said: 'I like it up here – but I don't like the way I got here.'

Dorr raised his head a few inches and looked at me with his mouth slightly open. He had beautiful teeth, but they hadn't grown in his mouth. He said: 'I'm a busy man, brother. It was simpler than arguing. Have a drink?'

'Sure I'll have a drink,' I said.

He squeezed the cat's head gently between his two palms, then pushed it away from him and put both hands down on the arms of his chair. He shoved hard and his face got a little red and he finally got up on his feet. He waddled across to a built-in cabinet and took out a squat decanter of whisky and two gold-veined glasses.

'No ice today,' he said, waddling back to the desk. 'Have to drink it straight.'

He poured two drinks, gestured, and I went over and got mine. He sat down again. I sat down with my drink. Dorr lit a long brown cigar, pushed the box two inches in my direction, leaned back and stared at me with complete relaxation.

'You're the guy that fingered Manny Tinnen,' he said. 'It won't do.'

I sipped my whisky. It was good enough to sip.

'Life gets complicated at times,' Dorr went on, in the same even, relaxed voice. 'Politics – even when it's a lot of fun – is tough on the nerves. You know me. I'm tough and I get what I want. There ain't a hell of a lot I want any more, but what I want – I want bad. And ain't so damn particular how I get it.'

'You have that reputation,' I said politely.

Dorr's eyes twinkled. He looked around for the cat, dragged it towards him by the tail, pushed it down on its side and began to rib its stomach. The cat seemed to like it.

Dorr looked at me and said very softly: 'You bumped Lou Harger.'

'What makes you think so?' I asked, without any particular emphasis.

'You bumped Lou Harger. Maybe he needed the bump – but you gave it to him. He was shot once through the heart, with a thirty-eight. You wear a thirty-eight and you're known to be a fancy shot with it. You were with Harger at Las Olindas last night and saw him win a lot of money. You were supposed to be acting as bodyguard for him, but you got a better idea. You caught up with him and that girl in West Cimarron, slipped Harger the dose and got the money.'

I finished my whisky, got up and poured myself some more of it.

'You made a deal with the girl,' Dorr said, 'but the deal didn't stick. She got a cute idea. But that don't matter, because the police got your gun along with Harger. And you got the dough.'

I said: 'Is there a tag out for me?'

'Not till I give the word . . . And the gun hasn't been turned in . . . I got a lot of friends, you know.'

I said slowly: 'I got coshed outside Canales' place. It served me right. My gun was taken from me. I never caught up with Harger, never saw him again. The girl came to me this morning with the money in an envelope and a story that Harger had been killed in her apartment. That's how I have the money – for safe keeping. I wasn't sure about the girl's story, but her bringing the money carried a lot of weight. And Harger was a friend of mine. I started out to investigate.'

'You should have let the cops do that,' Dorr said with a grin.

'There was a chance the girl was being framed. Besides there was a possibility I might make a few dollars – legitimately. It has been done, even in San Angelo.'

Dorr stuck a finger towards the cat's face and the cat bit it, with an absent expression. Then it pulled away from him, sat down on a corner of the desk and began to lick one toe.

'Twenty-two grand, and the jane passed it over to you to keep,' Dorr said. 'Ain't that just like a jane?'

'You got the dough,' Dorr said. 'Harger was killed with your gun. The girl's gone – but I could bring her back. I think she'd make a good witness, if we needed one.'

'Was the play at Las Olindas crooked?' I asked.

Dorr finished his drink and curled his lips around his cigar again. 'Sure,' he said carelessly. 'The croupier – a guy named Pina – was in on it. The wheel was wired for the double-zero. The old crap. Copper button on the floor, copper button on Pina's shoe sole, wires up his leg, batteries in his hip pockets. The old crap.'

I said: 'Canales didn't act as if he knew about it.'

Dorr chuckled. 'He knew the wheel was wired. He didn't know his head croupier was playin' on the other team.'

'I'd hate to be Pina,' I said.

Dorr made a negligent motion with his cigar. 'He's taken care of . . . The play was careful and quiet. They didn't make any fancy long shots, just even money bets, and they didn't win all the time. They couldn't. No wired wheel is that good.'

I shrugged, moved around in my chair. 'You know a hell of a lot about it,' I said. 'Was all this just to get me set for a squeeze?'

He grinned softly. 'Hell, no! Some of it just happened – the way the best plants do.' He waved his cigar again, and a pale grey tendril of smoke curled past his cunning little eyes. There was a muffled sound of talk in the outside room. 'I got connections I got to please – even if I don't like all their capers,' he added simply.

'Like Manny Tinnen?' I said. 'He was around City Hall a lot, knew too much. Okay, Master Dorr. Just what do you figure on having me do for you? Commit suicide?'

He laughed. His fat shoulders shook cheerfully. He put one of his small hands out with the palm towards me. 'I wouldn't think of that,' he said dryly, 'and the other way's better business. The way public opinion is about the Shannon kill, I ain't sure that louse of a DA wouldn't convict Tinnen without you – if he could sell the folks the idea you'd been knocked off to button your mouth.'

I got up out of my chair, went over and leaned on the desk, leaned across it towards Dorr.

He said: 'No funny business!' a little sharply and breathlessly. His hand went to a drawer and got it half open. His movements with his hands were very quick in contrast with the movements of his body.

I smiled down at the hand and he took it away from the drawer. I saw a gun just inside the drawer.

I said: 'I've already talked to the Grand Jury.'

Dorr leaned back and smiled at me. 'Guys make mistakes,' he said. 'Even smart private dicks . . . You could have a change of heart – and put it in writing.'

I said very softly: 'No. I'd be under a perjury rap – which I couldn't beat. I'd rather be under a murder rap – which I can beat. Especially as Fenweather will *want* me to beat it. He won't want to spoil me as a witness. The Tinnen case is too important to him.'

Dorr said evenly: 'Then you'll have to try and beat it, brother. And after you get through beating it there'll still be enough mud on your neck so no jury'll convict Manny on your say-so alone.'

I put my hand out slowly and scratched the cat's ear. 'What about the twenty-two grand?'

'It *could* be all yours, if you want to play. After all it ain't my money . . . If Manny gets clear, I might add a little something that *is* my money.'

I tickled the cat under its chin. It began to purr. I picked it up and held it gently in my arms.

'Who did kill Lou Harger, Dorr?' I asked, not looking at him.

He shook his head. I looked at him, smiling. 'Swell cat you have,' I said.

Dorr licked his lips. 'I think the little bastard likes you,' he grinned. He looked pleased at the idea.

I nodded – and threw the cat in his face.

He yelped, but his hands came up to catch the cat. The cat

twisted neatly in the air and landed with both front paws working. One of them split Dorr's cheek like a banana peel. He yelled very loudly.

I had the gun out of the drawer and the muzzle of it into the back of Dorr's neck when Beasley and the square-faced man dodged in.

For an instant there was a sort of tableau. Then the cat tore itself loose from Dorr's arms, shot to the floor and went under the desk. Beasley raised his snub-nosed gun, but he didn't look as if he was certain what he meant to do with it.

I shoved the muzzle of mine hard into Dorr's neck and said: 'Frankie gets it first, boys ... And that's not a gag.'

Dorr grunted in front of me. 'Take it easy,' he growled to his hoods. He took a handkerchief from his breast pocket and began to dab at his split and bleeding cheek with it. The man with the crooked mouth began to sidle along the wall.

I said: 'Don't get the idea I'm enjoying this, but I'm not fooling either. You heels stay put.'

The man with the crooked mouth stopped sidling and gave me a nasty leer. He kept his hands low.

Dorr half turned his head and tried to talk over his shoulder to me. I couldn't see enough of his face to get any expression, but he didn't seem scared. He said: 'This won't get you anything. I could have you knocked off easy enough, if that was what I wanted. Now where are you? You can't shoot anybody without getting in a worse jam than if you did what I asked you to. It looks like a stalemate to me.'

I thought that over for a moment while Beasley looked at me quite pleasantly, as though it was all just routine to him. There was nothing pleasant about the other man. I listened hard, but the rest of the house seemed to be quite silent.

Dorr edged forward from the gun and said: 'Well?'

I said: 'I'm going out. I have a gun and it looks like a gun that I could hit somebody with, if I have to. I don't want to very much, and if you'll have Beasley throw my keys over and the other one turn back the gun he took from me, I'll forget about the snatch.'

Dorr moved his arms in the lazy beginning of a shrug. 'Then what?'

'Figure out your deal a little closer,' I said. 'If you get enough protection behind me, I might throw in with you ... And if you're as tough as you think you are, a few hours won't cut any ice one way or the other.'

'It's an idea,' Dorr said and chuckled. Then to Beasley: 'Keep your rod to yourself and give him his keys. Also his gun – the one you got today.'

Beasley sighed and very carefully inserted a hand into his pants. He tossed my leather keycase across the room near the end of the desk. The man with the twisted mouth put his hand up, edged it inside his side pocket and I eased down behind Dorr's back, while he did it. He came out with my gun, let it fall to the floor and kicked it away from him.

I came out from behind Dorr's back, got my keys and the gun up from the floor, moved sidewise towards the door of the room. Dorr watched with an empty stare that meant nothing. Beasley followed me around with his body and stepped away from the door as I neared it. The other man had trouble holding himself quiet.

I got to the door and reversed a key that was in it. Dorr said dreamily: 'You're just like one of those rubber balls on the end of an elastic. The farther you get away, the suddener you'll bounce back.'

I said: 'The elastic might be a little rotten,' and went through the door, turned the key in it and braced myself for shots that didn't come. As a bluff, mine was thinner than the gold on a week-end wedding ring. It worked because Dorr let it and that was all.

I got out of the house, got the Marmon started and wangled it around and sent it skidding past the shoulder of the hill and so on down to the highway. There was no sound of anything coming after me.

When I reached the concrete highway bridge it was a little past two o'clock, and I drove with one hand for a while and wiped the sweat off the back of my neck.

Eight

The morgue was at the end of a long and bright and silent corridor that branched off from behind the main lobby of the County Building. The corridor ended in two doors and a blank wall faced with marble. One door had INQUEST ROOM lettered on a glass panel behind which there was no light. The other opened into a small, cheerful office.

A man with gander-blue eyes and rust-coloured hair parted in the exact centre of his head was pawing over some printed forms at a table. He looked up, looked me over, and then suddenly smiled.

I said: 'Hello, Landon ... Remember the Shelby case?'

The bright blue eyes twinkled. He got up and came around the table with his hand out. 'Sure. What can we do—' He broke off suddenly and snapped his fingers. 'Hell! You're the guy that put the bee on that hot rod.'

I tossed a butt through the open door into the corridor. 'That's not why I'm here,' I said. 'Anyhow not this time. There's a fellow named Louis Harger ... picked up shot last night or this morning, in West Cimarron, as I get it. Could I take a look-see?'

'They can't stop you,' Landon said.

He led the way through a door on the far side of his office into a place that was all white paint and white enamel and glass and bright light. Against one wall was a double tier of large bins with glass windows in them. Through the peepholes showed bundles in white sheeting, and, further back, frosted pipes.

A body covered with a sheet lay on a table that was high at the head and sloped down to the foot. Landon pulled the sheet down casually from a man's dead, placid, yellowish face. Long black hair lay loosely on a small pillow, with the dankness of water still in it. The eyes were half open and stared incuriously at the ceiling.

I stepped close, looked at the face, Landon pulled the

sheet on down and rapped his knuckles on a chest that rang hollowly, like a board. There was a bullet hole over the heart.

'Nice clean shot,' he said.

I turned away quickly, got a cigarette out and rolled it around in my fingers. I stared at the floor.

'Who identified him?'

'Stuff in his pockets,' Landon said. 'We're checking his prints, of course. You know him?'

I said: 'Yes.'

Landon scratched the base of his chin softly with his thumb-nail. We walked back into the office and Landon went behind his table and sat down.

He thumbed over some papers, separated one from the pile and studied it for a moment.

He said: 'A sheriff's radio car found him at 12.35 a.m., on the side of the old road out of West Cimarron, a quarter of a mile from where the cut-off starts. That isn't travelled much, but the prowl car takes a slant down it now and then looking for petting parties.'

I said: 'Can you say how long he had been dead?'

'Not very long. He was still warm, and the nights are cool along there.'

I put my unlighted cigarette in my mouth and moved it up and down with my lips. 'And I bet you took a long thirty-eight out of him,' I said.

'How did you know that?' Landon asked quickly.

'I just guess. It's that sort of hole.'

He stared at me with bright, interested eyes. I thanked him, said I'd be seeing him, went through the door and lit my cigarette in the corridor. I walked back to the elevators and got into one, rode to the seventh floor, then went along another corridor exactly like the one below except that it didn't lead to the morgue. It led to some small, bare offices that were used by the District Attorney's investigators. Half-way along I opened a door and went into one of them.

Bernie Ohls was sitting humped loosely at a desk placed against the wall. He was the chief investigator Fenweather had told me to see, if I got into any kind of a jam. He was a medium-sized blond man with white eyebrows and an out-thrust, very deeply cleft chin. There was another desk against the other wall, a couple of hard chairs, a brass spittoon on a rubber mat and very little else.

Ohls nodded casually at me, got out of his chair and fixed the door latch. Then he got a flat tin of little cigars out of his desk, lit one of them, pushed the tin along the desk and stared at me along his nose. I sat down in one of the straight chairs and tilted it back.

Ohls said: 'Well?'

'It's Lou Harger,' I said. 'I thought maybe it wasn't.'

'The hell you did. I could have told you it was Harger.'

Somebody tried the handle of the door, then knocked. Ohls paid no attention. Whoever it was went away.

I said slowly: 'He was killed between eleven-thirty and twelve thirty-five. There was just time for the job to be done where he was found. There wasn't time for it to be done the way the girl said. There wasn't time for me to do it.'

Ohls said: 'Yeah. Maybe you could prove that. And then maybe you could prove a friend of yours didn't do it with your gun.'

I said: 'A friend of mine wouldn't be likely to do it with my gun – if he was a friend of mine.'

Ohls grunted, smiled sourly at me sidewise. He said: 'Most anyone would think that. That's why he might have done it.'

I let the legs of my chair settle to the floor. I stared at him.

'Would I come and tell you about the money and the gun – everything that ties me to it?'

Ohls said expressionlessly: 'You would – if you knew damn well somebody else had already told it for you.'

I said: 'Dorr wouldn't lose much time.'

I pinched my cigarette out and flipped it towards the brass cuspidor. Then I stood up.

'Okay. There's no tag out for me yet – so I'll go over and tell my story.'

Ohls said: 'Sit down a minute.'

I sat down. He took his little cigar out of his mouth and flung it away from him with a savage gesture. It rolled along the brown linoleum and smoked in the corner. He put his arms down on the desk and drummed with the fingers of both hands. His lower lip came forward and pressed his upper lip back against his teeth.

'Dorr probably knows you're here now,' he said. 'The only reason you ain't in the tank upstairs is they're not sure but it would be better to knock you off and take a chance. If Fenweather loses the election, I'll be all washed up – if I mess around with you.'

I said: 'If he convicts Manny Tinnen, he won't lose the election.'

Ohls took another of the little cigars out of the box and lit it. He picked his hat off the desk, fingered it a moment, put it on.

'Why'd the redhead give you that song and dance about the bump in her apartment, the stiff on the floor – all that hot comedy?'

'They wanted me to go over there. They figured I'd go to see if a gun was planted – maybe just to check up on her. That got me away from the busy part of town. They could tell better if the DA had any boys watching my blind side.'

'That's just a guess,' Ohls said sourly.

I said: 'Sure.'

Ohls swung his thick legs around, planted his feet hard and leaned his hands on his knees. The little cigar twitched in the corner of his mouth.

'I'd like to get to know some of these guys that let loose of twenty-two grand just to colour up a fairy-tale,' he said nastily.

I stood up again and went past him towards the door.

Ohls said: 'What's the hurry?'

I turned around and shrugged, looked at him blankly. 'You don't act very interested,' I said.

He climbed to his feet, said wearily: 'The hack driver's

most likely a dirty little crook. But it might just be Dorr's lads don't know he rates in this. Let's go get him while his memory's fresh.'

Nine

The Green Top Garage was on Deviveras, three blocks east of Main. I pulled the Marmon up in front of a fireplug and got out. Ohls slumped in the seat and growled: 'I'll stay here. Maybe I can spot a tail.'

I went into a huge echoing garage, in the inner gloom of which a few brand new paint jobs were splashes of sudden colour. There was a small, dirty, glass-walled office in the corner and a short man sat there with a derby hat on the back of his head and a red tie under his stubbled chin. He was whittling tobacco into the palm of his hand.

I said: 'You the dispatcher?'

'Yeah.'

'I'm looking for one of your drivers,' I said. 'Name of Tom Sneyd.'

He put down the knife and the plug and began to grind the cut tobacco between his two palms. 'What's the beef?' he asked cautiously.

'No beef. I'm a friend of his.'

'More friends, huh? . . . He works nights, mister . . . So he's gone I guess. Seventeen twenty-three Renfrew. That's over by Grey Lake.'

I said: 'Thanks. Phone?'

'No phone.'

I pulled a folded city map from an inside pocket and unfolded part of it on the table in front of his nose. He looked annoyed.

'There's a big one on the wall,' he growled, and began to pack a short pipe with his tobacco.'

'I'm used to this one,' I said. I bent over the spread map, looking for Renfrew Street. Then I stopped and looked suddenly at the face of the man in the derby. 'You remembered that address damn quick,' I said.

He put his pipe in his mouth, bit hard on it, and pushed two thick fingers into the pocket of his open vest.

'Couple other mugs was askin' for it a while back.'

I folded the map very quickly and shoved it back into my pocket as I went through the door. I jumped across the sidewalk, slid under the wheel and plunged at the starter.

'We're headed,' I told Bernie Ohls. 'Two guys got the kid's address there a while back. It might be—'

Ohls grabbed the side of the car and swore as we took the corner on squealing tyres. I bent forward over the wheel and drove hard. There was a red light at Central. I swerved into a corner service station, went through the pumps, popped out on Central and jostled through some traffic to make a right turn east again.

A coloured traffic cop blew a whistle at me and then stared hard as if trying to read the licence number. I kept on going.

Warehouses, a produce market, a big gas tank, more warehouses, railroad tracks, and two bridges dropped behind us. I beat three traffic signals by a hair and went through a fourth. Six blocks on I got the siren from a motor-cycle cop. Ohls passed me a bronze star and I flashed it out of the car, twisting it so the sun caught it. The siren stopped. The motor-cycle kept right behind us for another dozen blocks, then sheered off.

Grey Lake is an artificial reservoir in a cut between two groups of hills, on the east fringe of San Angelo. Narrow but expensively paved streets wind around in the hills, describing elaborate curves along their flanks for the benefit of a few cheap and scattered bungalows.

We plunged up into the hills, reading street signs on the run. The grey silk of the lake dropped away from us and the exhaust of the old Marmon roared between crumbling banks that shed dirt down on the unused sidewalks. Mongrel dogs quartered in the wild grass among the gopher holes.

Renfrew was almost at the top. Where it began there was a small neat bungalow in front of which a child in a diaper and nothing else fumbled around in a wire pen on a patch of lawn. Then there was a stretch without houses. Then there were two houses, then the road dropped, slipped in and out of sharp turns, went between banks high enough to put the whole street in shadow.

Then a gun roared around a bend ahead of us.

Ohls sat up sharply, said: 'Oh-oh! That's no rabbit gun,' slipped his service pistol out and unlatched the door on his side.

We came out of the turn and saw two more houses on the down side of the hill, with a couple of steep lots between them. A long grey car was slewed across the street in the space between the two houses. Its left front tyre was flat and both its front doors were wide open, like the spread ears of an elephant.

A small, dark-faced man was kneeling on both knees in the street beside the open right-hand door. His right arm hung loose from his shoulder and there was blood on the hand that belonged to it. With his other hand he was trying to pick up an automatic from the concrete in front of him.

I skidded the Marmon to a fast stop and Ohls tumbled out.

'Drop that, you!' he yelled.

The man with the limp arm snarled, relaxed, fell back against the running board, and a shot came from behind the car and snapped in the air not very far from my ear. I was out on the road by that time. The grey car was angled enough towards the houses so that I couldn't see any part of its left side except the open door. The shot seemed to come from about there. Ohls put two slugs into the door. I dropped, looked under the car and saw a pair of feet. I shot at them and missed.

About that time there was a thin but very sharp crack from the corner of the nearest house. Glass broke in the grey car.

The gun behind it roared and plaster jumped out of the corner of the house wall, above the bushes. Then I saw the upper part of a man's body in the bushes. He was lying downhill on his stomach and he had a light rifle to his shoulder.

He was Tom Sneyd, the taxi driver.

Ohls grunted and charged the grey car. He fired twice more into the door, then dodged down behind the hood. More explosions occurred behind the car. I kicked the wounded man's gun out of his way, slid past him and snaked a look over the gas tank. But the man behind had had too many angles to figure.

He was a big man in a brown suit and he made a clatter running hard for the lip of the hill between the two bungalows. Ohl's gun roared. The man whirled and snapped a shot without stopping. Ohls was in the open now. I saw his hat jerk off his head. I saw him stand squarely on well-spread feet, steady his pistol as if he was on the police range.

But the big man was already sagging. My bullet had drilled through his neck. Ohls fired at him very carefully and he fell and the sixth and last slug from his gun caught the man in the chest and twisted him around. The side of his head slapped the kerb with a sickening crunch.

We walked towards him from opposite ends of the car. Ohls leaned down, heaved the man over on his back. His face in death had a loose, amiable expression, in spite of the blood all over his neck. Ohls began to go through his pockets.

I looked back to see what the other one was doing. He wasn't doing anything but sitting on the running board holding his right arm against his side and grimacing with pain.

Tom Sneyd scrambled up the bank and came towards us.

Ohls said: 'It's a guy named Poke Andrews. I've seen him around the pool rooms.' He stood up and brushed off his knee. He had some odds and ends in his left hand. 'Yeah, Poke Andrews. Gun work by the day, hour or week. I guess there was a livin' in it – for a while.'

'It's not the guy that coshed me,' I said. 'But it's the guy I was looking at when I got coshed. And if the redhead was giving out any truth at all this morning, it's likely the guy that shot Lou Harger.'

Ohls nodded, went over and got his hat. There was a hole in the brim. 'I wouldn't be surprised at all,' he said, putting his hat on calmly.

Tom Sneyd stood in front of us with his little rifle held rigidly across his chest. He was hatless and coatless, and had sneakers on his feet. His eyes were bright and mad, and he was beginning to shake.

'I knew I'd get them babies!' he crowed. 'I knew I'd fix them lousy bastards!' Then he stopped talking and his face began to change colour. It got green. He leaned down slowly, dropped his rifle, put both his hands on his bent knees.

Ohls said: 'You better go lay down somewhere, buddy. If I'm any judge of colour, you're goin' to shoot your cookies.'

Ten

Tom Sneyd was lying on his back on a day bed in the front room of his little bungalow. There was a wet towel across his forehead. A little girl with honey-coloured hair was sitting beside him, holding his hand. A young woman with hair a couple of shades darker than the little girl's sat in the corner and looked at Tom Sneyd with tired ecstasy.

It was very hot when we came in. All the windows were shut and all the blinds down. Ohls opened a couple of front windows and sat down beside them, looked out towards the grey car. The dark Mexican was anchored to its steering wheel by his good wrist.

'It was what they said about my little girl,' Tom Sneyd said from under the towel. 'That's what sent me screwy. They said they'd come back and get her, if I didn't play with them.'

Ohls said: 'Okay, Tom. Let's have it from the start.' He

put one of his little cigars in his mouth, looked at Tom Sneyd doubtfully, and didn't light it.

I sat in a very hard Windsor chair and looked down at the cheap, new carpet.

'I was readin' a mag., waiting for time to eat and go to work,' Tom Sneyd said carefully. 'The little girl opened the door. They come in with guns on us, got us all in here and shut the windows. They pulled down all the blinds but one and the Mex sat by that and kept looking out. He never said a word. The big guy sat on the bed here and made me tell him all about last night – twice. Then he said I was to forget I'd met anybody or come into town with anybody. The rest was okay.'

Ohls nodded and said: 'What time did you first see this man here?'

'I didn't notice,' Tom Sneyd said. 'Say eleven-thirty, quarter to twelve. I checked in to the office at one-fifteen, right after I got my hack at the Carillon. It took us a good hour to make town from the beach. We was in the drugstore talkin' say fifteen minutes, maybe longer.'

'That figures back to around midnight when you met him,' Ohls said.

Tom Sneyd shook his head and the towel fell down over his face. He pushed it back up again.

'Well, no,' Tom Sneyd said. 'The guy in the drugstore told me he closed up at twelve. He wasn't closing up when we left.'

Ohls turned his head and looked at me without expression. He looked back at Tom Sneyd. 'Tell us the rest about the two gunmen,' he said.

'The big guy said most likely I wouldn't have to talk to anybody about it. If I did and talked right, they'd be back with some dough. If I talked wrong, they'd be back for my little girl.'

'Go on,' Ohls said. 'They're full of crap.'

'They went away. When I saw them go on up the street I got screwy. Renfrew is just a pocket – one of them graft jobs. It goes on around the hill half a mile, then stops. There's no way to get off it. So they had to come back this way ... I got my twenty-two, which is all the gun I have, and hid in the bushes. I got the tyre with the second shot. I guess they thought it was a blow-out. I missed with the next and that put 'em wise. They got guns loose. I got the Mex then, and the big guy ducked behind the car ... That's all there was to it. Then you come along.'

Ohls flexed his thick, hard fingers and smiled grimly at the girl in the corner. 'Who lives in the next house, Tom?'

'A man named Grandy, a motorman on the inter-urban. He lives all alone. He's at work now.'

'I didn't guess he was home,' Ohls grinned. He got up and went over and patted the little girl on the head. 'You'll have to come down and make a statement, Tom.'

'Sure.' Tom Sneyd's voice was tired, listless. 'I guess I lose my job, too, for rentin' out the hack last night.'

'I ain't so sure about that,' Ohls said softly. 'Not if your boss likes guys with a few guts to run his hacks.'

He patted the little girl on the head again, went towards the door and opened it. I nodded at Tom Sneyd and followed Ohls out of the house. Ohls said quietly: 'He don't know about the kill yet. No need to spring it in front of the kid.'

We went over to the grey car. We had got some sacks out of the basement and spread them over the late Andrews, weighted them down with stones. Ohls glanced that way and said absently: 'I got to get to where there's a phone pretty quick.'

He leaned on the door of the car and looked in at the Mexican. The Mexican sat with his head back and his eyes half-closed and a drawn expression on his brown face. His left wrist was shackled to the spider of the wheel.

'What's your name?' Ohls snapped at him.

'Luis Cadena,' the Mexican said it in a soft voice without opening his eyes any wider.

'Which one of you heels scratched the guy at West Cimarron last night?'

'No understand, *senor*,' the Mexican said purringly.

'Don't go dumb on me, spig,' Ohls said dispassionately. 'It

gets me sore.' He leaned on the window and rolled his little cigar around in his mouth.

The Mexican looked faintly amused and at the same time very tired. The blood on his right hand had dried black.

Ohls said: 'Andrews scratched the guy in a taxi at West Cimarron. There was a girl along. We got the girl. You have a lousy chance to prove you weren't in on it.'

Light flickered and died behind the Mexican's half-open eyes. He smiled with a glint of small white teeth.

Ohls said: 'What did he do with the gun?'

'No understand, *senor*.'

Ohls said: 'He's tough. When they get tough it scares me.'

He walked away from the car and scuffed some loose dirt from the sidewalk beside the sacks that draped the dead man. His toe gradually uncovered the contractor's stencil in the cement. He read it out loud: 'Dorr Paving and Construction Company, San Angelo. It's a wonder the fat louse wouldn't stay in his own racket.'

I stood beside Ohls and looked down the hill between the two houses. Sudden flashes of light darted from the windshields of cars going along the boulevard that fringed Gray Lake, far below.

Ohls said: 'Well?'

I said: 'The killers knew about the taxi – maybe – and the girl friend reached town with the swag. So it wasn't Canales' job. Canales isn't the boy to let anybody play around with twenty-two grand of his money. The redhead was in on the kill, and it was done for a reason.'

Ohls grinned. 'Sure. It was done so you could be framed for it.'

I said: 'It's a shame how little account some folks take of human life – or twenty-two grand. Harger was knocked off so I could be framed and the dough was passed to me to make the frame tighter.'

'Maybe they thought you'd highball,' Ohls grunted. 'That would sew you up right.'

I rolled a cigarette around in my fingers. 'That would have

been a little too dumb, even for me. What do we do now? Wait till the moon comes up so we can sing – or go down the hill and tell some more little white lies?'

Ohls spat on one of Poke Andrews' sacks. He said gruffly: 'This is county land here. I could take all this mess over to the sub-station at Solano and keep it hush-hush for a while. The hack driver would be tickled to death to keep it under the hat. And I've gone far enough so I'd like to get the Mex in the goldfish room with me personal.'

'I'd like it that way too,' I said. 'I guess you can't hold it down there for long, but you might hold it down long enough for me to see a fat boy about a cat.'

Eleven

It was late afternoon when I got back to the hotel. The clerk handed me a slip which read: 'Please phone F.D. as soon as possible.'

I went upstairs and drank some liquor that was in the bottom of a bottle. Then I phoned down for another pint, scraped my chin, changed clothes and looked up Frank Dorr's number in the book. He lived in a beautiful old house on Greenview Park Crescent.

I made myself a tall smooth one with a tinkle and sat down in an easy chair with the phone at my elbow. I got a maid first. Then I got a man who spoke Mister Dorr's name as though he thought it might blow up in his mouth. After him I got a voice with a lot of silk in it. Then I got a long silence and at the end of the silence I got Frank Dorr himself. He sounded glad to hear from me.

He said: 'I've been thinking about our talk this morning, and I have a better idea. Drop out and see me ... And you might bring that money along. You just have time to get it out of the bank.'

I said: 'Yeah. The safe-deposit closes at six. But it's not your money.'

I heard him chuckle. 'Don't be foolish. It's all marked, and I wouldn't want to have to accuse you of stealing it.'

I thought that over, and didn't believe it – about the currency being marked. I took a drink out of my glass and said: 'I *might* be willing to turn it over to the party I got it from – in your presence.'

He said: 'Well – I told you that party left town. But I'll see what I can do. No tricks, please.'

I said of course no tricks, and hung up. I finished my drink, called Von Ballin of the *Telegram*. He said the sheriff's people didn't seem to have any ideas about Lou Harger – or give a damn. He was a little sore that I still wouldn't let him use my story. I could tell from the way he talked that he hadn't got the doings over near Grey Lake.

I called Ohls, couldn't reach him.

I mixed myself another drink, swallowed half of it and began to feel it too much. I put my hat on, changed my mind about the other half of my drink, went down to my car. The early evening traffic was thick with householders riding home to dinner. I wasn't sure whether two cars tailed me or just one. At any rate nobody tried to catch up and throw a pineapple in my lap.

The house was a square two-storeyed place of old red brick, with beautiful grounds and a red brick wall with a white stone coping around them. A shiny black limousine was parked under the porte-cochère at the side. I followed a red-flagged walk up over two terraces, and a pale wisp of a man in a cutaway coat let me into a wide, silent hall with dark old furniture and a glimpse of garden at the end. He led me along that and along another hall at right angles and ushered me softly into a panelled study that was dimly lit against the gathering dusk. He went away, leaving me alone.

The end of the room was mostly open french windows,

through which a brass-coloured sky showed behind a line of quiet trees. In front of the trees a sprinkler swung slowly on a patch of velvety lawn that was already dark. There were large dim oils on the walls, a huge black desk with books across one end, a lot of deep lounging chairs, a heavy soft rug that went from wall to wall. There was a faint smell of good cigars and beyond that somewhere a smell of garden flowers and moist earth. The door opened and a youngish man in pince-nez came in, gave me a slight formal nod, looked around vaguely, and said that Mr Dorr would be there in a moment. He went out again, and I lit a cigarette.

In a little while the door opened again and Beasley came in, walked past me with a grin and sat down just inside the windows. Then Dorr came in and behind him Miss Glenn.

Dorr had his black cat in his arms and two lovely red scratches, shiny with collodion, down his right cheek. Miss Glenn had on the same clothes I had seen on her in the morning. She looked dark and drawn and spiritless, and she went past me as though she had never seen me before.

Dorr squeezed himself into the high-backed chair behind the desk and put the cat down in front of him. The cat strolled over to one corner of the desk and began to lick its chest with a long, sweeping, businesslike motion.

Dorr said: 'Well, well. Here we are,' and chuckled pleasantly.

The man in the cutaway came in with a tray of cocktails, passed them around, put the tray with the shaker down on a low table beside Miss Glenn. He went out again, closing the door as if he was afraid he might crack it.

We all drank and looked very solemn.

I said: 'We're all here but two. I guess we have a quorum.'

Dorr said: 'What's that?' sharply and put his head to one side.

I said: 'Lou Harger's in the morgue and Canales is dodging cops. Otherwise we're all here. All the interested parties.'

Miss Glenn made an abrupt movement, then relaxed suddenly and picked at the arm of her chair.

Dorr took two swallows of his cocktail, put the glass aside

and folded his small neat hands on the desk. His face looked a little sinister.

'The money,' he said coldly. 'I'll take charge of it now.'

I said: 'Not now or any other time. I didn't bring it.'

Dorr stared at me and his face got a little red. I looked at Beasley. Beasley had a cigarette in his mouth and his hands in his pockets and the back of his head against the back of his chair. He looked half asleep.

Dorr said softly, meditatively: 'Holding out, huh?'

'Yes,' I said grimly. 'While I have it I'm fairly safe. You overplayed your hand when you let me get my paws on it. I'd be a fool not to hold what advantage it gives me.'

Dorr said: 'Safe?' with a gently sinister intonation.

I laughed. 'Not safe from a frame,' I said. 'But the last one didn't click so well ... Not safe from being gun-walked again. But that's going to be harder next time too ... But fairly safe from being shot in the back and having you sue my estate for the dough.'

Dorr stroked the cat and looked at me under his eyebrows.

'Let's get a couple of more important things straightened out,' I said. 'Who takes the rap for Lou Harger?'

'What makes you so sure *you* don't?' Dorr asked nastily.

'My alibi's been polished up. I didn't know how good it was until I knew how close Lou's death could be timed. I'm clear now ... regardless of who turns in what gun with what fairy-tale ... And the lads that were sent to scotch my alibi ran into some trouble.'

Dorr said: 'That so?' without any apparent emotion.

'A thug named Andrews and a Mexican calling himself Luis Cadena. I daresay you've heard of them.'

'I don't know such people,' Dorr said sharply.

'Then it won't upset you to hear Andrews got very dead, and the law has Cadena.'

'Certainly not,' Dorr said. 'They were from Canales. Canales had Harger killed.'

I said: 'So that's your new idea. I think it's lousy.'

I leaned over and slipped my empty glass under my chair.

Miss Glenn turned her head towards me and spoke very gravely, as if it was very important to the future of the race for me to believe what she said: 'Of course – *of course* Canales had Lou killed . . . At least, the men he sent after us killed Lou.'

I nodded politely. 'What for? A packet of money they didn't get? They wouldn't have killed him. They'd have brought him in, brought both of you in. You arranged for that kill, and the taxi stunt was to sidetrack me, not to fool Canales' boys.'

She put her hand out quickly. Her eyes were shimmering. I went ahead.

'I wasn't very bright, but I didn't figure on anything so flossy. Who the hell would? Canales had no motive to gun Lou, unless it got back the money he had been gypped out of. Supposing he could know that quick he *had* been gypped.'

Dorr was licking his lips and quivering his chins and looking from one of us to the other with his small tight eyes. Miss Glenn said drearily: 'Lou knew all about the play. He planned it with the croupier, Pina. Pina wanted some getaway money, wanted to move on to Havana. Of course Canales would have got wise, but not too soon, if I hadn't got noisy and tough. *I* got Lou killed – but not the way you mean.'

I dropped an inch of ash off a cigarette I had forgotten all about. 'All right,' I said grimly. 'Canales takes the rap . . . And I suppose you two chisellers think that's all I care about . . . Where was Lou going to be when Canales was *supposed* to find out he'd been gypped?'

'He was going to be gone,' Miss Glenn said tonelessly. 'A damn long way off. And I was going to be gone with him.'

I said: 'Nerts! You seem to forget *I* know *why* Lou was killed.'

Beasley sat up in his chair and moved his right hand rather delicately towards his left shoulder. 'This wise guy bother you, chief?'

Dorr said: 'Not yet. Let him rant.'

I moved so that I faced a little more towards Beasley. The sky had gone dark outside and the sprinkler had been turned off. A damp feeling came slowly into the room. Dorr opened a cedar-wood box and put a long brown cigar in his mouth, bit the end off with a dry snap of his false teeth. There was the harsh noise of a match striking, then the slow, rather laboured puffing of his breath in the cigar.

He said slowly, through a cloud of smoke: 'Let's forget all this and make a deal about that money ... Manny Tinnen hung himself in his cell this afternoon.'

Miss Glenn stood up suddenly, pushing her arms straight down at her sides. Then she sank slowly down into the chair again, sat motionless. I said: 'Did he have any help?' Then I made a sudden, sharp movement – and stopped.

Beasley jerked a swift glance at me, but I wasn't looking at Beasley. There was a shadow outside one of the windows – a lighter shadow than the dark lawn and darker trees. There was a hollow, bitter, coughing plop; a thin spray of whitish smoke in the window.

Beasley jerked, rose halfway to his feet, then fell on his face with one arm doubled under him.

Canales stepped through the window, past Beasley's body, came three steps further, and stood silent, with a long, black, small-calibred gun in his hand, the larger tube of a silencer flaring from the end of it.

'Be very still,' he said. 'I am a fair shot – even with this elephant gun.'

His face was so white that it was almost luminous. His dark eyes were all smoke-grey iris, without pupils.

'Sound carries well at night, out of open windows,' he said tonelessly.

Dorr put both his hands down on the desk and began to pat it. The black cat put its body very low, drifted down over the end of the desk and went under a chair. Miss Glenn turned her head towards Canales very slowly, as if some kind of mechanism moved it.

Canales said: 'Perhaps you have a buzzer on that desk. If the door of the room opens, I shoot. It will give me a lot of pleasure to see blood come out of your fat neck.'

I moved the fingers of my right hand two inches on the arm

of my chair. The silenced gun swayed towards me and I stopped moving my fingers. Canales smiled very briefly under his angular moustache.

'You are a smart dicks' he said. 'I thought I had you right. But there are things about you I like.'

I didn't say anything. Canales looked back at Dorr. He said very precisely: 'I have been bled by your organization for a long time. But this is something else again. Last night I was cheated out of some money. But this is trivial too. I am wanted for the murder of this Harger. A man named Cadena has been made to confess that I hired him . . . That is just a little too much fix.'

Dorr swayed gently over his desk, put his elbows down hard on it, held his face in his small hands and began to shake. His cigar was smoking on the floor.

Canales said: 'I would like to get my money back, and I would like to get clear of this rap – but most of all I would like you to say something – so I can shoot you with your mouth open and see blood come out of it.'

Beasley's body stirred on the carpet. His hands groped a little. Dorr's eyes were agony trying not to look at him. Canales was rapt and blind in his act by this time. I moved my fingers a little more on the arm of my chair. But I had a long way to go.

Canales said: 'Pina has talked to me. I saw to that. You killed Harger. Because he was a secret witness against Manny Tinnen. The DA kept the secret, and the dick here kept it. But Harger could not keep it himself. He told his broad – and the broad told you . . . So the killing was arranged, in a way to throw suspicion with a motive on me. First on this dick, and if that wouldn't hold, on me.'

There was silence. I wanted to say something, but I couldn't get anything out. I didn't think anybody but Canales would ever again say anything.

Canales said: 'You fixed Pina to let Harger and his girl win my money. It was not hard – because I don't play my wheels crooked.'

Dorr had stopped shaking. His face lifted, stone-white, and turned towards Canales, slowly, like the face of a man about to have an epileptic fit. Beasley was up on one elbow. His eyes were almost shut but a gun was labouring upwards in his hand.

Canales leaned forward and began to smile. His trigger finger whitened at the exact moment Beasley's gun began to pulse and roar.

Canales arched his back until his body was a rigid curve. He fell stiffly forward, hit the edge of the desk and slid along it to the floor, without lifting his hands.

Beasley dropped his gun and fell down on his face again. His body got soft and his fingers moved fitfully, then were still.

I got motion into my legs, stood up and went to kick Canales' gun under the desk – senselessly. Doing this I saw that Canales had fired at least once, because Frank Dorr had no right eye.

He sat still and quiet, with his chin on his chest and a nice touch of melancholy on the good side of his face.

The door of the room came open and the secretary with the pince-nez slid in pop-eyed. He staggered back against the door, closing it again. I could hear his rapid breathing across the room.

He gasped: 'Is – is anything wrong?'

I thought that very funny, even then. Then I realized that he might be short-sighted and from where he stood Frank Dorr looked natural enough. The rest of it could have been just routine to Dorr's help.

I said: 'Yes – but we'll take care of it. Stay out of here.'

He said: 'Yes, sir,' and went out again. That surprised me so much that my mouth fell open. I went down the room and bent over the grey-haired Beasley. He was unconscious, but had a fair pulse. He was bleeding from the side, slowly.

Miss Glenn was standing up and looked almost as dopy as Canales had looked. She was talking to me quickly, in a brittle, very distinct voice: 'I didn't know Lou was to be killed, but

I couldn't have done anything about it anyway. They burned me with a branding iron – just for a sample of what I'd get. Look!'

I looked. She tore her dress down in front and there was a hideous burn on her chest almost between her two breasts.

I said: 'Okay, sister. That's nasty medicine. But we've got to have some law here now and an ambulance for Beasley.'

I pushed past her towards the telephone, shook her hand off my arm when she grabbed at me. She went on talking to my back in a thin, desperate voice.

'I thought they'd just hold Lou out of the way until after the trial. But they dragged him out of the cab and shot him without a word. Then the little one drove the taxi into town and the big one brought me up into the hills to a shack. Dorr was there. He told me how you had to be framed. He promised me the money, if I went through with it, and torture till I died, if I let them down.'

It occurred to me that I was turning my back too much to people. I swung around, got the telephone in my hands, still on the hook, and put my gun down on the desk.

'Listen! Give me a break,' she said wildly. 'Dorr framed it all with Pina, the croupier. Pina was one of the gang that got Shannon where they could fix him. I didn't—'

I said: 'Sure – that's all right. Take it easy.'

The room, the whole house seemed very still, as if a lot of people were hunched outside the door, listening.

'It wasn't a bad idea,' I said, as if I had all the time in the world. 'Lou was just a white chip to Frank Dorr. The play he figured put us both out as witnesses. But it was too elaborate, took in too many people. That sort always blows up in your face.'

'Lou was getting out of the state,' she said, clutching at her dress. 'He was scared. He thought the roulette trick was some kind of a pay-off to him.

I said: 'Yeah,' lifted the phone and asked for police headquarters.

The room door came open again then and the secretary

barged in with a gun. A uniformed chauffeur was behind him with another gun.

I said very loudly into the phone: 'This is Frank Dorr's house. There's been a killing . . .'

The secretary and the chauffeur dodged out again. I heard running in the hall. I clicked the phone, called the *Telegram* office and got Von Ballin. When I got through giving him the flash Miss Glenn was gone out of the window into the dark garden.

I didn't go after her. I didn't mind very much if she got away.

I tried to get Ohls, but they said he was still down at Solano. And by that time the night was full of sirens.

I had a little trouble, but not too much. Fenweather pulled too much weight. Not all of the story came out, but enough so that the City Hall boys in the two-hundred-dollar suits had their left elbows in front of their faces for some time.

Pina was picked up in Salt Lake City. He broke and implicated four others of Manny Tinnen's gang. Two of them were killed resisting arrest, the other two got life without parole.

Miss Glenn made a clean getaway and was never heard of again. I think that's about all, except that I had to turn the twenty-two grand over to the Public Administrator. He allowed me two hundred dollars fee and nine dollars and twenty cents mileage. Sometimes I wonder what he did with the rest of it.

The King in Yellow

George Millar, night auditor at the Carlton Hotel, was a dapper wiry little man, with a soft deep voice like a torch singer's. He kept it low, but his eyes were sharp and angry, as he said into the PBX mouthpiece: 'I'm very sorry. It won't happen again. I'll send up at once.'

He tore off the headpiece, dropped it on the keys of the switchboard and marched swiftly from behind the pebbled screen and out into the entrance lobby. It was past one and the Carlton was two-thirds residential. In the main lobby, down three shallow steps, lamps were dimmed and the night porter had finished tidying up. The place was deserted – a wide space of dim furniture, rich carpet. Faintly in the distance a radio sounded. Millar went down the steps and walked quickly towards the sound, turned through an archway and looked at a man stretched out on a pale green davenport and what looked like all the loose cushions in the hotel. He lay on his side dreamy-eyed and listened to the radio two yards away from him.

Millar barked: 'Hey, you! Are you the house dick here or the house cat?'

Steve Grayce turned his head slowly and looked at Millar. He was a long black-haired man, about twenty-eight, with deep-set silent eyes and a rather gentle mouth. He jerked a thumb at the radio and smiled. 'King Leopardi, George. Hear that trumpet tone. Smooth as an angel's wing, boy.'

'Swell! Go on back upstairs and get him out of the corridor!'

Steve Grayce looked shocked. 'What – again? I thought I had those birds put to bed long ago.' He swung his feet to the floor and stood up. He was at least a foot taller than Millar.

'Well, Eight-sixteen says no. Eight-sixteen says he's out in the hall with two of his stooges. He's dressed in yellow satin shorts and a trombone and he and his pals are putting on a jam session. And one of those hustlers Quillan registered in eight-eleven is out there truckin' for them. Now get on to it, Steve – and this time make it stick.'

Steve Grayce smiled wryly. He said: 'Leopardi doesn't belong here anyway. Can I use chloroform or just my black-jack?'

He stepped long legs over the pale green carpet, through the arch and across the main lobby to the single elevator that was open and lighted. He slid the doors shut and ran it up to Eight, stopped it roughly and stepped out into the corridor.

The noise hit him like a sudden wind. The walls echoed with it. Half a dozen doors were open and angry guests in night robes stood in them peering.

'It's OK, folks,' Steve Grayce said rapidly. 'This is absolutely the last act. Just relax.'

He rounded the corner and the hot music almost took him off his feet. Three men were lined up against the wall, near an open door from which light streamed. The middle one, the one with the trombone, was six feet tall, powerful and graceful, with a hairline moustache. His face was flushed and his eyes had an alcoholic glitter. He wore yellow satin shorts with large initials embroidered in black on the left leg – nothing more. His torso was tanned and naked.

The two with him were in pyjamas, the usual halfway-good-looking band boys, both drunk, but not staggering drunk. One jittered madly on a clarinet and the other on a tenor saxophone.

Back and forth in front of them, strutting, trucking, preening herself like a magpie, arching her arms and her eyebrows, bending her fingers back until the carmine nails almost touched her arms, a metallic blonde swayed and went to town on the music. Her voice was a throaty screech, without melody, as false as her eyebrows and as sharp as her nails. She wore high-heeled slippers and black pyjamas with a long purple sash.

Steve Grayce stopped dead and made a sharp downward motion with his hand. 'Wrap it up!' he snapped. 'Can it. Put it on ice. Take it away and bury it. The show's out. Scram now – scram!'

King Leopardi took the trombone from his lips and bellowed: 'Fanfare to a house dick!'

The three drunks blew a stuttering note that shook the walls. The girl laughed foolishly and kicked out. Her slipper caught Steve Grayce in the chest. He picked it out of the air, jumped towards the girl and took hold of her wrist.

'Tough, eh?' he grinned. 'I'll take you first.'

'Get him!' Leopardi yelled. 'Sock him low! Dance the gumheel on his neck!'

Steve swept the girl off her feet, tucked her under his arm and ran. He carried her as easily as a parcel. She tried to kick his legs. He laughed and shot a glance through a lighted doorway. A man's brown brogues lay under a bureau. He went on past that to a second lighted doorway, slammed through and kicked the door shut, turned far enough to twist the tabbed key in the lock. Almost at once a fist hit the door. He paid no attention to it.

He pushed the girl along the short passage past the bathroom, and let her go. She reeled away from him and put her back to the bureau, panting, her eyes furious. A lock of damp gold-dipped hair swung down over one eye. She shook her head violently and bared her teeth.

'How would you like to get vagged, sister?'

'Go to hell!' she spit out. 'The King's a friend of mine, see? You better keep your paws off me, copper.'

'You run the circuit with the boys?'

She spat at him again.

'How'd you know they'd be here?'

Another girl was sprawled across the bed, her head to the wall, tousled black hair over a white face. There was a tear in the leg of her pyjamas. She lay limp and groaned.

Steve said harshly: 'Oh, oh, the torn-pyjama act. It flops here, sister, it flops hard. Now listen, you kids. You can go to bed and stay till morning or you can take the bounce. Make up your minds.'

The black-haired girl groaned. The blonde said: 'You get out of my room, you damned gum-heel!'

She reached behind her and threw a hand mirror. Steve ducked. The mirror slammed against the wall and fell without breaking. The black-haired girl rolled over on the bed and said wearily: 'Oh, lay off. I'm sick.'

She lay with her eyes closed, the lids fluttering.

The blonde swivelled her hips across the room to a desk by the window, poured herself a full half-glass of Scotch in a water glass and gurgled it down before Steve could get to her. She choked violently, dropped the glass and went down on her hands and knees.

Steve said grimly: 'That's the one that kicks you in the face, sister.'

The girl crouched, shaking her head. She gagged once, lifted the carmine nails to paw at her mouth. She tried to get up, and her foot skidded out from under her and she fell down on her side and went fast asleep.

Steve sighed, went over and shut the window and fastened it. He rolled the black-haired girl over and straightened her on the bed and got the bedclothes from under her, tucked a pillow under her head. He picked the blonde bodily off the floor and dumped her on the bed and covered both girls to the chin. He opened the transom, switched off the ceiling light and unlocked the door. He relocked it from the outside, with a master-key on a chain.

'Hotel business,' he said under his breath. 'Phooey.'

The corridor was empty now. One lighted door still stood open. Its number was 815, two doors from the room the girls were in. Trombone music came from it softly – but not softly enough for 1.25 a.m.

Steve Grayce turned into the room, crowded the door shut with his shoulder and went along past the bathroom. King Leopardi was alone in the room.

The bandleader was sprawled out in an easy chair, with a

tall misted glass at his elbow. He swung the trombone in a tight circle as he played it and the lights danced in the horn.

Steve lit a cigarette, blew a plume of smoke and stared through it at Leopardi with a queer, half-admiring, half-contemptuous expression.

He said softly: 'Lights out, yellow-pants. You play a sweet trumpet and your trombone don't hurt either. But we can't use it here. I already told you that once. Lay off. Put that thing away.'

Leopardi smiled nastily and blew a stuttering raspberry that sounded like a devil laughing.

'Says you,' he sneered. 'Leopardi does what he likes, where he likes, when he likes. Nobody's stopped him yet, gumshoe. Take the air.'

Steve hunched his shoulders and went close to the tall dark man. He said patiently: 'Put that bazooka down, big-stuff. People are trying to sleep. They're funny that way. You're a great guy on a band shell. Everywhere else you're just a guy with a lot of jack and a personal reputation that stinks from here to Miami and back. I've got a job to do and I'm doing it. Blow that thing again and I'll wrap it around your neck.'

Leopardi lowered the trombone and took a long drink from the glass at his elbow. His eyes glinted nastily. He lifted the trombone to his lips again, filled his lungs with air and blew a blast that rocked the walls. Then he stood up very suddenly and smoothly and smashed the instrument down on Steve's head.

'I never did like house peepers,' he sneered. 'They smell like public toilets.'

Steve took a short step back and shook his head. He leered, slid forward on one foot and smacked Leopardi open handed. The blow looked light, but Leopardi reeled all the way across the room and sprawled at the foot of the bed, sitting on the floor, his right arm draped in an open suitcase.

For a moment neither man moved. Then Steve kicked the trombone away from him and squashed his cigarette in a glass tray. His black eyes were empty but his mouth grinned whitely.

'If you want trouble,' he said, 'I come from where they make it.'

Leopardi smiled, thinly, tautly, and his right hand came up out of the suitcase with a gun in it. His thumb snicked the safety catch. He held the gun steady, pointing.

'Make some with this,' he said, and fired.

The bitter roar of the gun seemed a tremendous sound in the closed room. The bureau mirror splintered and glass flew. A sliver cut Steve's cheek like a razor blade. Blood oozed in a small narrow line on his skin.

He left his feet in a dive. His right shoulder crashed against Leopardi's bare chest and his left hand brushed the gun away from him, under the bed. He rolled swiftly to his right and came up on his knees spinning.

He said thickly, harshly: 'You picked the wrong gee, brother.'

He swarmed on Leopardi and dragged him to his feet by his hair, by main strength. Leopardi yelled and hit him twice on the jaw and Steve grinned and kept his left hand twisted in the band-leader's long sleek black hair. He turned his hand and the head twisted with it and Leopardi's third punch landed on Steve's shoulder. Steve took hold of the wrist behind the punch and twisted that and the bandleader went down on his knees yowling. Steve lifted him by the hair again, let go of his wrist and punched him three times in the stomach, short terrific jabs. He let go of the hair then as he sank the fourth punch almost to his wrist.

Leopardi sagged blindly to his knees and vomited.

Steve stepped away from him and went into the bathroom and got a towel off the rack. He threw it at Leopardi, jerked the open suitcase on to the bed and started throwing things into it.

Leopardi wiped his face and got to his feet still gagging. He swayed, braced himself on the end of the bureau. He was white as a sheet.

Steve Grayce said: 'Get dressed, Leopardi. Or go out the way you are. It's all one to me.'

Leopardi stumbled into the bathroom, pawing the wall like a blind man.

Two

Millar stood very still behind the desk as the elevator opened. His face was white and scared and his cropped black moustache was a smudge across his upper lip. Leopardi came out of the elevator first, a muffler around his neck, a lightweight coat tossed over his arm, a hat tilted on his head. He walked stiffly, bent forward a little, his eyes vacant. His face had a greenish pallor.

Steve Grayce stepped out behind him carrying a suitcase, and Carl, the night porter, came last with two more suitcases and two instrument cases in black leather. Steve marched over to the desk and said harshly: 'Mr Leopardi's bill – if any. He's checking out.'

Millar goggled at him across the marble desk. 'I – I don't think, Steve—'

'OK I thought not.'

Leopardi smiled very thinly and unpleasantly and walked out through the brass-edged swing doors the porter held open for him. There were two nighthawk cabs in the line. One of them came to life and pulled up to the canopy and the porter loaded Leopardi's stuff into it. Leopardi got into the cab and leaned forward to put his head to the open window. He said slowly and thickly: 'I'm sorry for you, gumheel. I mean sorry.'

Steve Grayce stepped back and looked at him woodenly. The cab moved off down the street, rounded a corner and was gone. Steve turned on his heel, took a quarter from his pocket and tossed it up in the air. He slapped it into the night porter's hand.

'From the King,' he said. 'Keep it to show your grandchildren.'

He went back into the hotel, got into the elevator without looking at Millar, shot it up to Eight again and went along the corridor, master-keyed his way into Leopardi's room. He relocked it from the inside, pulled the bed out from the wall and went in behind it. He got a .32 automatic off the carpet, put it in his pocket and prowled the floor with his eyes looking for the ejected shell. He found it against the wastebasket, reached to pick it up, and stayed bent over, staring into the basket. His mouth tightened. He picked up the shell and dropped it absently into his pocket, then reached a questing finger into the basket and lifted out a torn scrap of paper on which a piece of newsprint had been pasted. Then he picked up the basket, pushed the bed back against the wall and dumped the contents of the basket out on it.

From the trash of torn papers and matches he separated a number of pieces with newsprint pasted to them. He went over to the desk with them and sat down. A few minutes later he had the torn scraps put together like a jigsaw puzzle and could read the message that had been made by cutting words and letters from magazines and pasting them on a sheet:

TEN GRAND BY THURSDAY NIGHT LEOPARDI.

DAY AFTER YOU OPEN AT THE CLUB SHALOTTE.

OR ELSE – CURTAINS. FROM HER BROTHER.

Steve Grayce said: 'Huh.' He scooped the torn pieces into an hotel envelope, put that in his inside breast pocket and lit a cigarette. 'The guy had guts,' he said. 'I'll grant him that – and his trumpet.'

He locked the room, listened a moment in the now silent corridor, then went along to the room occupied by the two girls. He knocked softly and put his ear to the panel. A chair squeaked and feet came towards the door.

'What is it?' The girl's voice was cool, wide awake. It was not the blonde's voice.

'The house man. Can I speak to you a minute?'

'You're speaking to me.'

'Without the door between, lady.'

'You've got the pass-key. Help yourself.' The steps went away. He unlocked the door with his master-key, stepped quietly inside and shut it. There was a dim light in a lamp with a shirred shade on the desk. On the bed the blonde snored heavily, one hand clutched in her brilliant metallic hair. The black-haired girl sat in the chair by the window, her legs crossed at right angles like a man's and stared at Steve emptily.

He went close to her and pointed to the long tear in her pyjama leg. He said softly: 'You're not sick. You were not drunk. That tear was done a long time ago. What's the racket? A shakedown on the King?'

The girl stared at him coolly, puffed at a cigarette and said nothing.

'He checked out,' Steve said. 'Nothing doing in that direction now, sister.' He watched her like a hawk, his black eyes hard and steady on her face.

'Aw, you house dicks make me sick!' the girl said with sudden anger. She surged to her feet and went past him into the bathroom, shut and locked the door.

Steve shrugged and felt the pulse of the girl asleep in the bed – a thumpy, draggy pulse, a liquor pulse.

'Poor damn hustlers,' he said under his breath.

He looked at a large purple bag that lay on the bureau, lifted it idly and let it fall. His face stiffened again. The bag made a heavy sound on the glass top, as if there were a lump of lead inside it. He snapped it open quickly and plunged a hand in. His fingers touched the cold metal of a gun. He opened the bag wide and stared down into it at a small .25 automatic. A scrap of white paper caught his eye. He fished it out and held it to the light – a rent receipt with a name and address. He stuffed it into his pocket closed the bag and was standing by the window when the girl came out of the bathroom.

'Hell, are you still haunting me?' she snapped. 'You know what happens to hotel dicks that master-key their way into ladies' bedrooms at night?'

Steve said loosely: 'Yeah. They get in trouble. They might even get shot at.'

The girl's face became set, but her eyes crawled sideways and looked at the purple bag. Steve looked at her. 'Know Leopardi in 'Frisco?' he asked. 'He hasn't played here in two years. Then he was just a trumpet player in Vane Utigore's band – a cheap outfit.'

The girl curled her lip, went past him and sat down by the window again. Her face was white, stiff. She said dully: 'Blossom did. That's Blossom on the bed.'

'Know he was coming to this hotel tonight?'

'What makes it your business?'

'I can't figure him coming here at all,' Steve said. 'This is a quiet place. So I can't figure anybody coming here to put the bite on him.'

'Go somewhere else and figure. I need sleep.'

Steve said: 'Good-night, sweetheart – and keep your door locked.'

A thin man with thin blond hair and thin face was standing by the desk, tapping on the marble with thin fingers. Millar was still behind the desk and he still looked white and scared. The thin man wore a dark grey suit with a scarf inside the collar of the coat. He had a look of having just got up. He turned sea-green eyes slowly on Steve as he got out of the elevator, waited for him to come up to the desk and throw a tabbed key on it.

Steve said: 'Leopardi's key, George. There's a busted mirror in his room and the carpet has his dinner on it – mostly Scotch.' He turned to the thin man. 'You want to see me, Mr Peters?'

'What happened, Grayce?' The thin man had a tight voice that expected to be lied to.

'Leopardi and two of his boys were on Eight, the rest of

the gang on Five. The bunch on Five went to bed. A couple of obvious hustlers managed to get themselves registered just two rooms from Leopardi. They managed to contact him and everybody was having a lot of nice noisy fun out in the hall. I could only stop it by getting a little tough.'

'There's blood on your cheek,' Peter said coldly. 'Wipe it off.'

Steve scratched at his cheek with a handkerchief. The thin thread of blood had dried. 'I got the girls tucked away in their room,' he said. 'The two stooges took the hint and holed up, but Leopardi still thought the guests wanted to hear trombone music. I threatened to wrap it around his neck and he beaned me with it. I slapped him open-handed and he pulled a gun and took a shot at me. Here's the gun.'

He took the .32 automatic out of his pocket and laid it on the desk. He put the used shell beside it. 'So I beat some sense into him and threw him out,' he added.

Peters tapped on the marble. 'Your usual tact seems to have been well in evidence.'

Steve stared at him. 'He shot at me,' he repeated quietly. 'With a gun. This gun. I'm tender to bullets. He missed, but suppose he hadn't? I like my stomach the way it is, with just one way in and one way out.'

Peters narrowed his tawny eyebrows. He said very politely: 'We have you down on the pay-roll here as a night clerk, because we don't like the name house detective. But neither night clerks nor house detectives put guests out of the hotel without consulting me. Not ever, Mr Grayce.'

Steve said: 'The guy shot at me, pal. With a gun. Catch on? I don't have to take that without a kickback, do I?' His face was a little white.

Peters said: 'Another point for your consideration. The controlling interest in this hotel is owned by Mr Halsey G. Walters. Mr Walters also owns the Club Shalotte, where King Leopardi is opening on Wednesday night. And that, Mr Grayce, is why Leopardi was good enough to give us his business. Can you think of anything else I should like to say to you?'

'Yeah. I'm canned,' Steve said mirthlessly.

'Very correct, Mr Grayce. Good-night, Mr Grayce.'

The thin blond man moved to the elevator and the night porter took him up.

Steve looked at Millar.

'Jumbo, Walters, huh?' he said softly. 'A tough, smart guy. Much too smart to think this dump and the Club Shalotte belong to the same sort of customers. Did Peters write Leopardi to come here?'

'I guess he did, Steve.' Millar's voice was low and gloomy.

'Then why wasn't he put in a tower suite with a private balcony to dance on, at twenty-eight bucks a day? Why was he put on a medium-priced transient floor? And why did Quillan let those girls get so close to him?'

Millar pulled at his black moustache. 'Tight with money – as well as with Scotch, I suppose. As to the girls, I don't know.'

Steve slapped the counter open-handed. 'Well, I'm canned, for not letting a drunken heel make a parlour house and a shooting gallery out of the eighth floor. Nuts! Well, I'll miss the joint at that.'

'I'll miss you too, Steve,' Millar said gently. 'But not for a week. I take a week off starting tomorrow. My brother has a cabin at Crestline.'

'Didn't know you had a brother,' Steve said absently. He opened and closed his fist on the marble desk top.

'He doesn't come into town much. A big guy. Used to be a fighter.'

Steve nodded and straightened from the counter. 'Well, I might as well finish out the night,' he said. 'On my back. Put this gun away somewhere, George.'

He grinned coldly and walked away, down the steps into the dim main lobby and across to the room where the radio was. He punched the pillows into shape on the pale green davenport, then suddenly reached into his pocket and took out the scrap of white paper he had lifted from the black-haired girl's purple handbag. It was a receipt for a week's rent, to a Miss Marilyn Delorme, Apt 211, Ridgeland Apartments, 118 Court Street.

He tucked it into his wallet and stood staring at the silent radio. 'Steve, I think you got another job,' he said under his breath. 'Something about this set-up smells.'

He slipped into a closetlike phone booth in the corner of the room, dropped a nickel and dialled an all-night radio station. He had to dial four times before he got a clear line to the Owl Programme announcer.

'How's to play King Leopardi's record of "Solitude" again?' he asked him.

'Got a lot of requests piled up. Played it twice already. Who's calling?'

'Steve Grayce, night man at the Carlton Hotel.'

'Oh, a sober guy on his job. For you, pal, anything.'

Steve went back to the davenport, snapped the radio on and lay down on his back, with his hands clasped behind his head.

Ten minutes later the high, piercingly sweet trumpet notes of King Leopardi came softly from the radio, muted almost to a whisper, and sustaining E above high C for an almost incredible period of time.

'Shucks,' Steve grumbled, when the record ended. 'A guy that can play like that – maybe I was too tough with him.'

Three

Court Street was old town, wop town, crook town, arty town. It lay across the top of Bunker Hill and you could find anything there from down at heels ex-Greenwich-villagers to crooks on the lam, from ladies of anybody's evening to County Relief clients brawling with haggard landladies in grand old houses with scrolled porches, parquetry floors, and immense sweeping banisters of white oak, mahogany and Circassian walnut.

It had been a nice place once, had Bunker Hill, and from the days of its niceness there still remained the funny little funicular railway, called the Angel's Flight, which crawled up and down a yellow clay bank from Hill Street. It was afternoon when Steve Grayce got off the car at the top, its only passenger. He walked along in the sun, a tall, wide-shouldered, rangy-looking man in a well-cut blue suit.

He turned west at Court and began to read the numbers. The one he wanted was two from the corner, across the street from a red brick funeral parlour with a sign in gold over it: PAOLO PERRUGINI FUNERAL HOME. A swarthy iron-grey Italian in a cutaway coat stood in front of the curtained door of the red brick building, smoking a cigar and waiting for somebody to die.

One-eighteen was a three-storeyed frame apartment house. It had a glass door, well masked by a dirty net curtain, a hall runner eighteen inches wide, dim doors with numbers painted on them with dim paint, a staircase halfway back. Brass stair rods glittered in the dimness of the hallway.

Steve Grayce went up the stairs and prowled back to the front. Apartment 211, Miss Marilyn Delorme, was on the right, a front apartment. He tapped lightly on the wood, waited, tapped again. Nothing moved beyond the silent door, or in the hallway. Behind another door across the hall somebody coughed and kept on coughing.

Standing there in the half-light Steve Grayce wondered why he had come. Miss Delorme had carried a gun. Leopardi had received some kind of a threat letter and torn it up and thrown it away. Miss Delorme had checked out of the Carlton about an hour after Steve told her Leopardi was gone. Even at that—

He took out a leather keyholder and studied the lock of the door. It looked as if it would listen to reason. He tried a pick on it, snicked the bolt back and stepped softly into the room. He shut the door, but the pick wouldn't lock it.

The room was dim with drawn shades across two front windows. The air smelled of face powder. There was light-painted furniture, a pull-down double bed which was pulled down but had been made up. There was a magazine on it, a glass tray full of cigarette butts, a pint bottle half full of whisky, and a glass on a chair beside the bed. Two pillows had been used for a back rest and were still crushed in the middle.

On the dresser there was a composition toilet set, neither cheap nor expensive, a comb with black hair in it, a tray of manicuring stuff, plenty of spilled powder – in the bathroom, nothing. In a closet behind the bed a lot of clothes and two suitcases. The shoes were all one size.

Steve stood beside the bed and pinched his chin. 'Blossom, the spitting blonde, doesn't live here,' he said under his breath. 'Just Marilyn the torn-pants brunette.'

He went back to the dresser and pulled drawers out. In the bottom drawer, under the piece of wallpaper that lined it, he found a box of .25 copper-nickel automatic shells. He poked at the butts in the ashtray. All had lipstick on them. He pinched his chin again, then feathered the air with the palm of his hand, like an oarsman with a scull.

'Bunk,' he said softly. 'Wasting your time, Stevie.'

He walked over to the door and reached for the knob, then turned back to the bed and lifted it by the footrail.

Miss Marilyn Delorme was in.

She lay on her side on the floor under the bed, long legs scissored out as if in running. One mule was on, one off. Garters and skin showed at the tops of her stockings, and a blue rose on something pink. She wore a square-necked, short-sleeved dress that was not too clean. Her neck above the dress was blotched with purple bruises.

Her face was a dark plum colour, her eyes had the faint stale glitter of death, and her mouth was open so far that it foreshortened her face. She was colder than ice, and still quite limp. She had been dead two or three hours at least, six hours at most.

The purple bag was beside her, gaping like her mouth. Steve didn't touch any of the stuff that had been emptied out on the floor. There was no gun and there were no papers.

He let the bed down over her again, then made the rounds of the apartment, wiping everything he had touched and a lot of things he couldn't remember whether he had touched or not.

He listened at the door and stepped out. The hall was still empty. The man behind the opposite door still coughed. Steve went down the stairs, looked at the mailboxes and went back along the lower hall to a door.

Behind this door a chair creaked monotonously. He knocked and a woman's sharp voice called out. Steve opened the door with his handkerchief and stepped in.

In the middle of the room a woman rocked in an old Boston rocker, her body in the slack boneless attitude of exhaustion. She had a mud-coloured face, stringy hair, grey cotton stockings – everything a Bunker Hill landlady should have. She looked at Steve with the interested eye of a dead goldfish.

'Are you the manager?'

The woman stopped rocking, screamed: 'Hi, Jake! Company!' at the top of her voice, and started rocking again.

An icebox door thudded shut behind a partly open inner door and a very big man came into the room carrying a can of beer. He had a doughy mooncalf face, a tuft of fuzz on top of an otherwise bald head, a thick brutal neck and chin, and brown pig eyes about as expressionless as the woman's. He needed a shave – had needed one the day before – and his collarless shirt gaped over a big hard hairy chest. He wore scarlet suspenders with large gilt buckles on them.

He held the can of beer out to the woman. She clawed it out of his hand and said bitterly: 'I'm so tired I ain't got no sense.'

The man said: 'Yah. You ain't done the halls so good at that.'

The woman snarled: 'I done 'em as good as I aim to.' She sucked the beer thirstily.

Steve looked at the man and said: 'Manager?'

'Yah. 'S me. Jake Stoyanoff. Two hun'erd eighty-six stripped, and still plenty tough.'

Steve said: 'Who lives in Two-eleven?'

The big man leaned forward a little from the waist and snapped his suspenders. Nothing changed in his eyes. The skin along his big jaw may have tightened a little. 'A dame,' he said.

'Alone?'

'Go on – ask me,' the big man said. He stuck his hand out and lifted a cigar off the edge of a stained-wood table. The cigar was burning unevenly and it smelled as if somebody had set fire to the doormat. He pushed it into his mouth with a hard, thrusting motion, as if he expected his mouth wouldn't want it to go in.

'I'm asking you,' Steve said.

'Ask me out in the kitchen,' the big man drawled.

He turned and held the door open. Steve went past him.

The big man kicked the door shut against the squeak of the rocking chair, opened up the icebox and got out two cans of beer. He opened them and handed one to Steve.

'Dick?'

Steve drank some of the beer, put the can down on the sink, got a brand new card out of his wallet – a business card printed that morning. He handed it to the man.

The man read it, put it down on the sink, picked it up and read it again. 'One of them guys,' he growled over his beer. 'What's she pulled this time?'

Steve shrugged and said: 'I guess it's the usual. The torn-pyjama act. Only there's a kickback this time.'

'How come? You handling it, huh? Must be a nice cosy one.'

Steve nodded. The big man blew smoke from his mouth. 'Go ahead and handle it,' he said.

'You don't mind a pinch here?'

The big man laughed heartily. 'Nuts to you, brother,' he said pleasantly enough. 'You're a private dick. So it's a hush. OK. Go out and hush it. And if it *was* a pinch – that bothers me like a quart of milk. Go into your act. Take all the room you want. Cops don't bother Jake Stoyanoff.'

Steve stared at the man. He didn't say anything. The big man talked it up some more, seemed to get more interested. 'Besides,' he went on, making motions with the cigar, 'I'm softhearted. I never turn up a dame. I never put a frill in the middle.' He finished his beer and threw the can in a basket under the sink, and pushed his hand out in front of him, revolving the large thumb slowly against the next two fingers. 'Unless there's some of that,' he added.

Steve said softly: 'You've got big hands. You could have done it.'

'Huh?' His small brown leathery eyes got silent and stared.

Steve said: 'Yeah. You might be clean. But with those hands the cops'd go round and round with you just the same.'

The big man moved a little to his left, away from the sink. He let his right hand hang down at his side, loosely. His mouth got so tight that the cigar almost touched his nose.

'What's the beef, huh?' he barked. 'What you shovin' at me, guy? What—'

'Cut it,' Steve drawled. 'She's been croaked. Strangled. Upstairs, on the floor under her bed. About mid-morning, I'd say. Big hands did it – hands like yours.'

The big man did a nice job of getting the gun off his hip. It arrived so suddenly that it seemed to have grown in his hand and been there all the time.

Steve frowned at the gun and didn't move. The big man looked him over. 'You're tough,' he said. 'I been in the ring long enough to size up a guy's meat. You're plenty hard, boy. But you ain't as hard as lead. Talk it up fast.'

'I knocked at her door. No answer. The lock was a push-over. I went in. I almost missed her because the bed was pulled down and she had been sitting on it, reading a magazine. There was no sign of struggle. I lifted the bed just before I left – and there she was. Very dead, Mr Stoyanoff. Put the gat away. Cops don't bother you, you said a minute ago.'

The big man whispered: 'Yes and no. They don't make me

happy neither. I get a bump once'n a while. Mostly a Dutch. You said something about my hands, mister.'

Steve shook his head. 'That was a gag,' he said. 'Her neck has nail marks. You bite your nails down close. You're clean.'

The big man didn't look at his fingers. He was very pale. There was sweat on his lower lips, in the black stubble of his beard. He was still leaning forward, still motionless, when there was a knocking beyond the kitchen door, the door from the living-room to the hallway. The creaking chair stopped and the woman's sharp voice screamed: 'Hi, Jake! Company!'

The big man cocked his head. 'That old slut couldn't climb off'n her seat if the house caught fire,' he said thickly.

He stepped to the door and slipped through it, locking it behind him.

Steve ranged the kitchen swiftly with his eyes. There was a small high window beyond the sink, a trap down for a garbage pail and parcels, but no other door. He reached for his card Stoyanoff had left lying on the drainboard and slipped it back into his pocket. Then he took a short-barrelled Detective Special out of his left breast pocket where he wore it nose down, as in a holster.

He had got that far when the shots roared beyond the wall – muffled a little, but still loud – four of them blended in a blast of sound.

Steve stepped back and hit the kitchen door with his leg out straight. It held and jarred him to the top of his head and in his hip joint. He swore, took the whole width of the kitchen and slammed into it with his left shoulder. It gave this time. He pitched into the living-room. The mud-faced woman sat leaning forward in her rocker, her head to one side and a lock of mousy hair smeared down over her bony forehead.

'Backfire, huh?' she said stupidly. 'Sounded kinda close. Musta been in the alley.'

Steve jumped across the room, yanked the outer door open and plunged out into the hall.

The big man was still on his feet, a dozen feet down the

hallway, in the direction of a screen door that opened flush on an alley. He was clawing at the wall. His gun lay at his feet. His left knee buckled and he went down on it.

A door was flung open and a hard-looking woman peered out, and instantly slammed her door shut again. A radio suddenly gained in volume beyond her door.

The big man got up off his left knee and the leg shook violently inside his trousers. He went down on both knees and got the gun into his hand and began to crawl towards the screen door. Then, suddenly he went down flat on his face and tried to crawl that way, grinding his face into the narrow hall runner.

Then he stopped crawling and stopped moving altogether. His body went limp and the hand holding the gun opened and the gun rolled out of it.

Steve hit the screen door and was out in the alley. A grey sedan was speeding towards the far end of it. He stopped, steadied himself and brought his gun up level, and the sedan whisked out of sight around the corner.

A man boiled out of another apartment house across the alley. Steve ran on, gesticulating back at him and pointing ahead. As he ran he slipped the gun back into his pocket. When he reached the end of the alley, the grey sedan was out of sight. Steve skidded around the wall on to the sidewalk, slowed to a walk and then stopped.

Half a block down a man finished parking a car, got out and went across the sidewalk to a lunchroom. Steve watched him go in, then straightened his hat and walked along the wall to the lunchroom.

He went in, sat at the counter and ordered coffee. In a little while there were sirens.

Steve drank his coffee, asked for another cup and drank that. He lit a cigarette and walked down the long hill to Fifth, across to Hill, back to the foot of the Angel's Flight, and got his convertible out of a parking lot.

He drove out west, beyond Vermont, to the small hotel where he had taken a room that morning.

Four

Bill Dockery, floor manager of the Club Shalotte, teetered on his heels and yawned in the unlighted entrance to the dining-room. It was a dead hour for business, late cocktail time, too early for dinner, and much too early for the real business of the club, which was high-class gambling.

Dockery was a handsome mug in a midnight-blue dinner jacket and a maroon carnation. He had a two-inch forehead under black lacquer hair, good features a little on the heavy side, alert brown eyes and very long curly eyelashes which he liked to let down over his eyes, to fool troublesome drunks into taking a swing at him.

The entrance door of the foyer was opened by the uniformed doorman and Steve Grayce came in.

Dockery said: 'Ho, hum,' tapped his teeth and leaned his weight forward. He walked across the lobby slowly to meet the guest. Steve stood just inside the doors and ranged his eyes over the high foyer walled with milky glass, lighted softly from behind. Moulded in the glass were etchings of sailing ships, beasts of the jungle, Siamese pagodas, temples of Yucatan. The doors were square frames of chromium, like photo frames. The Club Shalotte had all the class there was, and the mutter of voices from the bar lounge on the left was not noisy. The faint Spanish music behind the voice was delicate as a carved fan.

Dockery came up and leaned his sleek head forward an inch. 'May I help you?'

'King Leopardi around?'

Dockery leaned back again. He looked less interested. 'The bandleader? He opens tomorrow night.'

'I thought he might be around – rehearsing or something.'

'Friend of his?'

'I know him. I'm not job-hunting, and I'm not a song plugger if that's what you mean.'

Dockery teetered on his heels. He was tone-deaf, and

Leopardi meant no more to him than a bag of peanuts. He half smiled. 'He was in the bar lounge a while ago.' He pointed with his square rock-like chin. Steve Grayce went into the bar lounge.

It was about a third full, warm and comfortable and not too dark nor too light. The little Spanish orchestra was in an archway, playing with muted strings small seductive melodies that were more like memories than sounds. There was no dance floor. There was a long bar with comfortable seats, and there were small round composition-top tables, not too close together. A wall seat ran around three sides of the room. Waiters flitted among the tables like moths.

Steve Grayce saw Leopardi in the far corner, with a girl. There was an empty table on each side of him. The girl was a knockout.

She looked tall and her hair was the colour of a brush fire seen through a dust cloud. On it, at the ultimate rakish angle, she wore a black velvet double-pointed beret with two artificial butterflies made of polka-dotted feathers and fastened on with tall silver pins. Her dress was burgundy-red wool and the blue fox draped over one shoulder was at least two feet wide. Her eyes were large, smoke-blue, and looked bored. She slowly turned a small glass on the table top with a gloved left hand.

Leopardi faced her, leaning forward, talking. His shoulders looked very big in a shaggy, cream-coloured sports coat. Above the neck of it his hair made a point on his brown neck. He laughed across the table as Steve came up, and his laugh had a confident, sneering sound.

Steve stopped, then moved behind the next table. The movement caught Leopardi's eye. His head turned, he looked annoyed, and then his eyes got very wide and brilliant and his whole body turned slowly, like a mechanical toy.

Leopardi put both his rather small well-shaped hands down on the table, on either side of a highball glass. He smiled. Then he pushed his chair back and stood up. He put one finger up and touched his hairline moustache, with theatrical delicacy. Then he said drawlingly, but distinctly: 'You son of a bitch!'

A man at a nearby table turned his head and scowled. A waiter who had started to come over stopped in his tracks, then faded back among the tables. The girl looked at Steve Grayce and then leaned back against the cushions of the wall seat and moistened the end of one bare finger on her right hand and smoothed a chestnut eyebrow.

Steve stood quite still. There was a sudden high flush on his cheekbones. He said softly: 'You left something at the hotel last night. I think you ought to do something about it. Here.'

He reached a folded paper out of his pocket and held it out. Leopardi took it, still smiling, opened it and read it. It was a sheet of yellow paper with torn pieces of white paper pasted on it. Leopardi crumpled the sheet and let it drop at his feet.

He took a smooth step towards Steve and repeated more loudly: 'You son of a bitch!'

The man who had first looked around stood up sharply and turned. He said clearly: 'I don't like that sort of language in front of my wife.'

Without even looking at the man Leopardi said: 'To hell with you and your wife.'

The man's face got a dusky red. The woman with him stood up and grabbed a bag and a coat and walked away. After a moment's indecision the man followed her. Everybody in the place was staring now. The waiter who had faded back among the tables went through the doorway into the entrance foyer, walking very quickly.

Leopardi took another, longer step and slammed Steve Grayce on the jaw. Steve rolled with the punch and stepped back and put his hand down on another table and upset a glass. He turned to apologize to the couple at the table. Leopardi jumped forward very fast and hit him behind the ear.

Dockery came through the doorway, split two waiters like a banana skin and started down the room showing all his teeth.

Steve gagged a little and ducked away. He turned and said thickly: 'Wait a minute, you fool – that isn't all of it – there's—'

Leopardi closed in fast and smashed him full on the mouth. Blood oozed from Steve's lip and crawled down the line at the corner of his mouth and glistened on his chin. The girl with the red hair reached for her bag, white-faced with anger, and started to get up from behind her table.

Leopardi turned abruptly on his heel and walked away. Dockery put out a hand to stop him. Leopardi brushed it aside and went on, went out of the lounge.

The tall red-haired girl put her bag down on the table again and dropped her handkerchief on the floor. She looked at Steve quietly, spoke quietly. 'Wipe the blood off your chin before it drips on your shirt.' She had a soft, husky voice with a trill in it.

Dockery came up harsh-faced, took Steve by the arm and put weight on the arm. 'All right, you! Let's go!'

Steve stood quite still, his feet planted, staring at the girl. He dabbed at his mouth with a handkerchief. He half smiled. Dockery couldn't move him an inch. Dockery dropped his hand, signalled two waiters and they jumped behind Steve, but didn't touch him.

Steve felt his lip carefully and looked at the blood on his handkerchief. He turned to the people at the table behind him and said: 'I'm terribly sorry. I lost my balance.'

The girl whose drink he had spilled was mopping her dress with a small fringed napkin. She smiled up at him and said: 'It wasn't your fault.'

The two waiters suddenly grabbed Steve's arms from behind. Dockery shook his head and they let go again. Dockery said tightly: 'You hit him?'

'No.'

'You say anything to make him hit you?'

'No.'

The girl at the corner table bent down to get her fallen handkerchief. It took her quite a time. She finally got it and slid into the corner behind the table again. She spoke coldly.

'Quite right, Bill. It was just some more of the King's sweet way with his public.'

Dockery said 'Huh?' and swivelled his head on his thick hard neck. Then he grinned and looked back at Steve.

Steve said grimly: 'He gave me three good punches, one from behind, without a return. You look pretty hard. See can you do it.'

Dockery measured him with his eyes. He said evenly: 'You win. I couldn't . . . Beat it!' he added sharply to the waiters. They went away. Dockery sniffed his carnation, and said quietly: 'We don't go for brawls in here.' He smiled at the girl again and went away, saying a word here and there at the tables. He went out through the foyer doors.

Steve tapped his lip, put his handkerchief in his pocket and stood searching the floor with his eyes.

The red-haired girl said calmly: 'I think I have what you want in my handkerchief. Won't you sit down?'

Her voice had a remembered quality, as if he had heard it before.

He sat down opposite her, in the chair where Leopardi had been sitting.

The red-haired girl said: 'The drink's on me. I was with him.'

Steve said: 'Coke with a dash of bitters,' to the waiter.

The waiter said: 'Madame?'

'Brandy and soda. Light on the brandy, please.' The waiter bowed and drifted away. The girl said amusedly: 'Coke with a dash of bitters. That's what I love about Hollywood. You meet so many neurotics.'

Steve stared into her eyes and said softly: 'I'm an occasional drinker, the kind of guy who goes out for a beer and wakes up in Singapore with a full beard.'

'I don't believe a word of it. Have you known the King long?'

'I met him last night. I didn't get along with him.'

'I sort of noticed that.' She laughed. She had a rich low laugh, too.

'Give me that paper, lady.'

'Oh, one of these impatient men. Plenty of time.' The handkerchief with the crumpled yellow sheet inside it was clasped tightly in her gloved hand. Her middle right finger played with an eyebrow. 'You're not in pictures, are you?'

'Hell, no.'

'Same here. Me, I'm too tall. The beautiful men have to wear stilts in order to clasp me to their bosoms.'

The waiter set the drinks down in front of them, made a grace note in the air with his napkin and went away.

Steve said quietly, stubbornly: 'Give me that paper, lady.'

'I don't like that "lady" stuff. It sounds like cop to me.'

'I don't know your name.'

'I don't know yours. Where did you meet Leopardi?'

Steve sighed. The music from the little Spanish orchestra had a melancholy minor sound now and the muffled clicking of grouds dominated it.

Steve listened to it with his head on one side. He said: 'The E string is a half-tone flat. Rather cute effect.'

The girl stared at him with new interest. I'd never have noticed that,' she said. 'And I'm supposed to be a pretty good singer. But you haven't answered my question.'

He said slowly: 'Last night I was house dick at the Carlton Hotel. They called me night clerk, but house dick was what I was. Leopardi stayed there and cut up too rough. I threw him out and got canned.'

The girl said: 'Ah. I begin to get the idea. He was being the King and you were being – if I might guess – a pretty tough order of house detective.'

'Something like that. Now will you please—'

'You still haven't told me your name.'

He reached for his wallet, took one of the brand new cards out of it and passed it across the table. He sipped his drink while she read it.

'A nice name,' she said slowly. 'But not a very good address. And *Private investigator* is bad. It should have been *Investigations*, very small, in the lower left-hand corner.'

'They'll be small enough,' Steve grinned. 'Now will you please—'

She reached suddenly across the table and dropped the crumpled ball of paper in his hand.

'Of course I haven't read it – and of course I'd like to. You do give me that much credit, I hope' – she looked at the card again, and added – 'Steve. Yes, and your office should be in a Georgian or very modernistic building in the Sunset Eighties. Suite Something-or-other. And your clothes should be very jazzy. Very jazzy indeed, Steve. To be inconspicuous in this town is to be a busted flush.'

He grinned at her. His deep-set black eyes had lights in them. She put the card away in her bag, gave her fur piece a yank, and drank about half of her drink. 'I have to go.' She signalled the waiter and paid the check. The waiter went away and she stood up.

Steve said sharply: 'Sit down.'

She stared at him wonderingly. Then she sat down again and leaned against the wall, still staring at him. Steve leaned across the table, asked: 'How well do *you* know Leopardi?'

'Off and on for years. If it's any of your business. Don't go masterful on me, for God's sake. I loathe masterful men. I once sang for him, but not for long. You can't just sing for Leopardi – if you get what I mean.'

'You were having a drink with him.'

She nodded slightly and shrugged. 'He opens here tomorrow night. He was trying to talk me into singing for him again. I said no, but I may have to, for a week or two anyway. The man who owns the Club Shalotte also owns my contract – and the radio station where I work a good deal.'

'Jumbo Walters,' Steve said. 'They say he's tough but square. I never met him, but I'd like to. After all I've got a living to get. Here.'

He reached back across the table and dropped the crumpled paper. 'The name was—'

'Dolores Chiozza.'

Steve repeated it lingeringly. 'I like it. I like your singing too. I've heard a lot of it. You don't oversell a song, like most of these high-money torchers.' His eyes glistened.

The girl spread the paper on the table and read it slowly, without expression. Then she said quietly: 'Who tore it up?'

'Leopardi, I guess. The pieces were in his wastebasket last night. I put them together, after he was gone. The guy has guts – or else he gets these things so often they don't register any more.'

'Or else he thought it was a gag.' She looked across the table levelly, then folded the paper and handed it back.

'Maybe. But if he's the kind of guy I hear he is – one of them is going to be on the level and the guy behind it is going to do more than just shake him down.'

Dolores Chiozza said: 'He's the kind of guy you hear he is.'

'It wouldn't be hard for a woman to get to him then – would it – a woman with a gun?'

She went on staring at him. 'No. And everybody would give her a big hand, if you ask me. If I were you, I'd just forget the whole thing. If he wants protection – Walters can throw more around him than the police. If he doesn't – who cares? I don't. I'm damn sure I don't.'

'You're kind of tough yourself, Miss Chiozza – over some things.'

She said nothing. Her face was a little white and more than a little hard.

Steve finished his drink, pushed his chair back and reached for his hat. He stood up. 'Thank you very much for the drink, Miss Chiozza. Now that I've met you I'll look forward all the more to hearing you sing again.'

'You're damn formal all of a sudden,' she said.

He grinned. 'So long, Dolores.'

'So long, Steve. Good luck – in the sleuth racket. If I hear of anything—'

He turned and walked among the tables out of the bar lounge.

Five

In the crisp fall evening the lights of Hollywood and Los Angeles winked at him. Searchlight beams probed the cloudless sky as if searching for bombing-planes.

Steve got his convertible out of the parking lot and drove it east along Sunset. At Sunset and Fairfax he bought an evening paper and pulled over to the kerb to look through it. There was nothing in the paper about 118 Court Street.

He drove on and ate dinner at the little coffee shop beside his hotel and went to a movie. When he came out he bought a home edition of the *Tribune*, a morning sheet. They were in that – both of them.

Police thought Jake Stoyanoff might have strangled the girl, but she had not been attacked. She was described as a stenographer, unemployed at the moment. There was no picture of her. There was a picture of Stoyanoff that looked like a touched-up police photo. Police were looking for a man who had been talking to Stoyanoff just before he was shot. Several people said he was a tall man in a dark suit. That was all the description the police got – or gave out.

Steve grinned sourly, stopped at the coffee shop for a good-night cup of coffee and then went up to his room. It was a few minutes to eleven o'clock. As he unlocked his door the telephone started to ring.

He shut the door and stood in the darkness remembering where the phone was. Then he walked straight to it, catlike in the dark room, sat in an easy chair and reached the phone up from the lower shelf of a small table. He held the one-piece to his ear and said: 'Hello.'

'Is this Steve?' It was a rich, husky voice, low, vibrant. It held a note of strain.

'Yeah, this is Steve. I can hear you. I know who you are.'

There was a faint dry laugh. 'You'll make a detective after all. And it seems I'm to give you your first case. Will you come over to my place at once? It's Twenty-four-twelve

Renfrew – North, there isn't any South – just half a block below Fountain. It's a sort of bungalow court. My house is the last in line, at the back.'

Steve said: 'Yes. Sure. What's the matter?'

There was a pause. A horn blared in the street outside the hotel. A wave of white light went across the ceiling from some car rounding the corner uphill. The low voice said very slowly: 'Leopardi. I can't get rid of him. He's – he's passed out in my bedroom.' Then a tinny laugh that didn't go with the voice at all.

Steve held the phone so tight his hand ached. His teeth clicked in the darkness. He said flatly, in a dull, brittle voice: 'Yeah. It'll cost you twenty bucks.'

'Of course. Hurry, please.'

He hung up, sat there in the dark room breathing hard. He pushed his hat back on his head, then yanked it forward again with a vicious jerk and laughed out loud. 'Hell,' he said, '*that* kind of a dame.'

Twenty-four-twelve Renfrew was not strictly a bungalow court. It was a staggered row of six bungalows, all facing the same way, but so arranged that no two of their front entrances overlooked each other. There was a brick wall at the back and beyond the brick wall a church. There was a long smooth lawn, moon-silvered.

The door was up two steps, with lanterns on each side and an ironwork grill over the peephole. This opened to his knock and a girl's face looked out, a small oval face with a Cupid's bow mouth, arched and plucked eyebrows, wavy brown hair. The eyes were like two fresh and shiny chestnuts.

Steve dropped a cigarette and put his foot on it. 'Miss Chiozza. She's expecting me. Steve Grayce.'

'Miss Chiozza has retired, sir,' the girl said with a half-insolent twist to her lips.

'Break it up, kid. You heard me, I'm expected.'

The wicket slammed shut. He waited, scowling back along the narrow moonlit lawn towards the street. OK. So it was like that – well, twenty bucks was worth a ride in the moonlight anyway.

The lock clicked and the door opened wide. Steve went past the maid into a warm cheerful room, old-fashioned with chintz. The lamps were neither old nor new and there were enough of them – in the right places. There was a hearth behind a panelled copper screen, a davenport close to it, a bar-top radio in the corner.

The maid said stiffly: 'I'm sorry, sir. Miss Chiozza forgot to tell me. Please have a chair.' The voice was soft, and it might be cagey. The girl went off down the room – short skirts, sheer silk stockings, and four-inch spike heels.

Steve sat down and held his hat on his knee and scowled at the wall. A swing door creaked shut. He got a cigarette out and rolled it between his fingers and then deliberately squeezed it to a shapeless flatness of white paper and ragged tobacco. He threw it away from him, at the fire screen.

Dolores Chiozza came towards him. She wore green velvet lounging pyjamas with a long gold-fringed sash. She spun the end of the sash as if she might be going to throw a loop with it. She smiled a slight artificial smile. Her face had a clean scrubbed look and her eyelids were bluish and they twitched.

Steve stood up and watched the green morocco slippers peep out under the pyjamas as she walked. When she was close to him he lifted his eyes to her face and said dully: 'Hello.'

She looked at him very steadily, then spoke in a high, carrying voice. 'I know it's late, but I knew you were used to being up all night. So I thought what we had to talk over – Won't you sit down?'

She turned her head very slightly, seemed to be listening for something.

Steve said: 'I never go to bed before two. Quite all right.'

She went over and pushed a bell beside the hearth. After a moment the maid came through the arch.

'Bring some ice cubes, Agatha. Then go along home. It's getting pretty late.'

'Yes'm.' The girl disappeared.

There was a silence then that almost howled till the tall girl took a cigarette absently out of a box, put it between her lips and Steve struck a match clumsily on his shoe. She pushed the end of the cigarette into the flame and her smoke-blue eyes were very steady on his black ones. She shook her head very slightly.

The maid came back with a copper ice bucket. She pulled a low Indian-brass tray-table between them before the davenport, put the ice bucket on it, then a siphon, glasses and spoons, and a triangular bottle that looked like good Scotch had come in it except that it was covered with silver filigree work and fitted with a stopper.

Dolores Chiozza said: 'Will you mix a drink?' in a formal voice.

He mixed two drinks, stirred them, handed her one. She sipped it, shook her head. 'Too light,' she said. He put more whisky in it and handed it back. She said, 'Better,' and leaned back against the corner of the davenport.

The maid came into the room again. She had a small rakish red hat on her wavy brown hair and was wearing a grey coat trimmed with nice fur. She carried a black brocade bag that could have cleaned out a fair-sized icebox. She said: 'Good-night, Miss Dolores.'

'Good-night, Agatha.'

The girl went out the front door, closed it softly. Her heels clicked down the walk. A car door opened and shut distantly and a motor started. Its sound soon dwindled away. It was a very quiet neighbourhood.

Steve put his drink down on the brass tray and looked levelly at the tall girl, said harshly: 'That means she's out of the way?'

'Yes. She goes home in her own car. She drives me home from the studio in mine – when I go to the studio, which I did tonight. I don't like to drive a car myself.'

'Well, what are you waiting for?'

The red-haired girl looked steadily at the panelled fire-screen and the unlit log fire behind it. A muscle twitched in her cheek.

After a moment she said: 'Funny that I called you instead of Walters. He'd have protected me better than you can. Only he wouldn't have believed me. I thought perhaps you would. I didn't invite Leopardi here. So far as I know – we two are the only people in the world who know he's here.'

Something in her voice jerked Steve upright.

She took a small crisp handkerchief from the breast pocket of the green velvet pyjama suit, dropped it on the floor, picked it up swiftly and pressed it against her mouth. Suddenly, without making a sound, she began to shake like a leaf.

Steve said swiftly: 'What the hell – I can handle that heel in my hip pocket. I did last night – and last night he had a gun and took a shot at me.'

Her head turned. Her eyes were very wide and staring. 'But it couldn't have been my gun,' she said in a dead voice.

'Huh? Of course not – what—?'

'It's my gun tonight,' she said and stared at him. 'You said a woman could get to him with a gun very easily.'

He just stared at her. His face was white now and he made a vague sound in his throat.

'He's not drunk, Steve,' she said gently. 'He's dead. In yellow pyjamas – in my bed. With my gun in his hand. You didn't think he was just drunk – did you, Steve?'

He stood up in a swift lunge, then became absolutely motionless, staring down at her. He moved his tongue on his lips and after a long time he formed words with it. 'Let's go look at him,' he said in a hushed voice.

Six

The room was at the back of the house to the left. The girl took a key out of her pocket and unlocked the door. There was a low light on a table, and the venetian blinds were drawn. Steve went in past her silently, on cat feet.

Leopardi lay squarely in the middle of the bed, a large smooth silent man, waxy and artificial in death. Even his moustache looked phoney. His half-open eyes, sightless as marbles, looked as if they had never seen. He lay on his back, on the sheet, and the bedclothes were thrown over the foot of the bed.

The King wore yellow silk pyjamas, the slip-on kind, with a turned collar. They were loose and thin. Over his breast they were dark with blood that had seeped into the silk as if into blotting-paper. There was a little blood on his bare brown neck.

Steve stared at him and said tonelessly: 'The King in Yellow. I read a book with that title once. He liked yellow, I guess. I packed some of his stuff last night. And he wasn't yellow either. Guys like him usually are – or are they?'

The girl went over to the corner and sat down in a slipper chair and looked at the floor. It was a nice room, as modernistic as the living-room was casual. It had a chenille rug, café-au-lait colour, severely angled furniture in inlaid wood, and a trick dresser with a mirror for a top, a kneehole and drawers like a desk. It had a box mirror above and a semi-cylindrical frosted wall-light set above the mirror. In the corner there was a glass table with a crystal greyhound on top of it, and a lamp with the deepest drum shade Steve had ever seen.

He stopped looking at all this and looked at Leopardi again. He pulled the King's pyjamas up gently and examined the wound. It was directly over the heart and the skin was scorched and mottled there. There was not so very much blood. He had died in a fraction of a second.

A small Mauser automatic lay cuddled in his right hand, on top of the bed's second pillow.

'That's artistic,' Steve said and pointed. 'Yeah, that's a nice touch. Typical contact wound, I guess. He even pulled his pyjama shirt up. I've heard they do that. A Mauser .763 about. Sure it's your gun?'

'Yes.' She kept on looking at the floor. 'It was in a desk in the living-room – not loaded. But these shells. I don't know why. Somebody gave it to me once. I didn't even know how to load it.'

Steve smiled. Her eyes lifted suddenly and she saw his smile and shuddered. 'I don't expect anybody to believe that,' she said. 'We may as well call the police, I suppose.'

Steve nodded absently, put a cigarette in his mouth and flipped it up and down with his lips that were still puffy from Leopardi's punch. He lit a match on his thumbnail, puffed a small plume of smoke and said quietly: 'No cops. Not yet. Just tell it.'

The red-haired girl said: 'I sing at KFQC, you know. Three nights a week – on a quarter-hour automobile programme. This was one of the nights. Agatha and I got home – oh, close to half-past ten. At the door I remembered there was no soda-water in the house, so I sent her back to the liquor store three blocks away, and came in alone. There was a queer smell in the house. I don't know what it was. As if several men had been in here, somehow. When I came in the bedroom – he was exactly as he is now. I saw the gun and I went and looked and then I knew I was sunk. I didn't know what to do. Even if the police cleared me, everywhere I went from now on—'

Steve said sharply: 'He got in here – how?'

'I don't know.'

'Go on,' he said.

'I locked the door. Then I undressed – with that on my bed. I went into the bathroom to shower and collect my brains, if any. I locked the door when I left the room and took the key. Agatha was back then, but I don't think she saw me.

Well, I took the shower and it braced me up a bit. Then I had a drink and then I came in here and called you.'

She stopped and moistened the end of a finger and smoothed the end of her left eyebrow with it. 'That's all, Steve – absolutely all.'

'Domestic help can be pretty nosy. This Agatha's nosier than most – or I miss my guess.' He walked over to the door and looked at the lock. 'I bet there are three or four keys in the house that knock this over.' He went to the windows and felt the catches, looked down at the screens through the glass. He said over his shoulder, casually: 'Was the King in love with you?'

Her voice was sharp, almost angry. 'He never was in love with any woman. A couple of years back in San Francisco, when I was with his band for a while, there was some slap-silly publicity about us. Nothing to it. It's been revived here in the hand-outs to the press, to build up his opening. I was telling him this afternoon I wouldn't stand for it, that I wouldn't be linked with him in anybody's mind. His private life was filthy. It reeked. Everybody in the business knows that. And it's not a business where daisies grow very often.'

Steve said: 'Yours was the only bedroom he couldn't make?'

The girl flushed to the roots of her dusky red hair.

'That sounds lousy,' he said. 'But I have to figure the angles. That's about true, isn't it?'

'Yes. I suppose so. I wouldn't say the only one.'

'Go on out in the other room and buy yourself a drink.'

She stood up and looked at him squarely across the bed. 'I didn't kill him, Steve. I didn't let him into this house tonight. I didn't know he was coming here, or had any reason to come here. Believe that or not. But something about this is wrong. Leopardi was the last man in the world to take his lovely life himself.'

Steve said: 'He didn't, angel. Go buy that drink. He was murdered. The whole thing is a frame – to get a cover-up from Jumbo Walters. Go on out.

He stood silent, motionless, until sounds he heard from

the living-room told him she was out there. Then he took out his handkerchief and loosened the gun from Leopardi's right hand and wiped it over carefully on the outside, broke out the magazine and wiped that off, spilled out all the shells and wiped every one, ejected the one in the breech and wiped that. He reloaded the gun and put it back in Leopardi's dead hand and closed his fingers around it and pushed his index finger against the trigger. Then he let the hand fall naturally back on the bed.

He pawed through the bedclothes and found an ejected shell and wiped that off, put it back where he had found it. He put the handkerchief to his nose, sniffed it wryly, went around the bed to a clothes closet and opened the door.

'Careless of your clothes, boy,' he said softly.

The rough cream-coloured coat hung in there, on a hook, over dark grey slacks with a lizard-skin belt. A yellow satin shirt and a wine-coloured tie dangled alongside. A handkerchief to match the tie flowed loosely four inches from the breast pocket of the coat. On the floor lay a pair of gazelle-leather nutmeg-brown sports shoes, and socks without garters. And there were yellow satin shorts with heavy black initials on them lying close by.

Steve felt carefully in the grey slacks and got out a leather key-holder. He left the room, went along the cross-hall and into the kitchen. It had a solid door, a good spring lock with a key stuck in it. He took it out and tried keys from the bunch in the key-holder, found none that fitted, put the other key back and went into the living-room. He opened the front door, went outside and shut it again without looking at the girl huddled in a corner of the davenport. He tried keys in the lock, finally found the right one. He let himself back into the house, returned to the bedroom and put the keyholder back in the pocket of the grey slacks again. Then he went to the living-room.

The girl was still huddled motionless, staring at him.

He put his back to the mantel and puffed at a cigarette. 'Agatha with you all the time at the studio?'

She nodded. 'I suppose so. So he had a key. That was what you were doing, wasn't it?'

'Yes. Had Agatha long?'

'About a year.'

'She steal from you? Small stuff, I mean?'

Dolores Chiozza shrugged wearily. 'What does it matter? Most of them do. A little face cream or powder, a handkerchief, a pair of stockings once in a while. Yes, I think she stole from me. They look on that sort of thing as more or less legitimate.'

'Not the nice ones, angel.'

'Well – the hours were a little trying. I work at night, often get home very late. She's a dresser as well as a maid.'

'Anything else about her? She use cocaine or weed? Hit the bottle? Ever have laughing fits?'

'I don't think so. What has she got to do with it, Steve?'

'Lady, she sold somebody a key to your apartment. That's obvious. You didn't give him one, the landlord wouldn't give him one, but Agatha had one. Check?'

Her eyes had a stricken look. Her mouth trembled a little, not much. A drink was untasted at her elbow. Steve bent over and drank some of it.

She said slowly: 'We're wasting time, Steve. We have to call the police. There's nothing anybody can do. I'm done for as a nice person, even if not as a lady at large. They'll think it was a lovers' quarrel and I shot him and that's that. If I could convince them I didn't, then he shot himself in my bed, and I'm still ruined. So I might as well make up my mind to face the music.'

Steve said softly: 'Watch this. My mother used to do it.'

He put a finger to his mouth, bent down and touched her lips at the same spot with the same finger. He smiled, said: 'We'll go to Walters – or you will. He'll pick his cops and the ones he picks won't go screaming through the night with reporters sitting in their laps. They'll sneak in quiet, like process servers. Walters can handle this. That was what was counted on. Me, I'm going to collect Agatha. Because I want a description of the guy she sold that key to – and I want it fast. And by the way, you owe me twenty bucks for coming over here. Don't let that slip your memory.'

The tall girl stood up, smiling. 'You're a kick, you are,' she said. 'What makes you so sure he was murdered?'

'He's not wearing his own pyjamas. His have his initials on them. I packed his stuff last night – before I threw him out of the Carlton. Get dressed, angel – and get me Agatha's address.'

He went into the bedroom and pulled a sheet over Leopardi's body, held it a moment above the still, waxen face before letting it fall.

'So long, guy,' he said gently. 'You were a louse – but you sure had music in you.'

It was a small frame house on Brighton Avenue near Jefferson, in a block of small frame houses, all old-fashioned, with front porches. This one had a narrow concrete walk which the moon made whiter than it was.

Steve mounted the steps and looked at the light-edged shade of the wide front window. He knocked. There were shuffling steps and a woman opened the door and looked at him through the hooked screen – a dumpy elderly woman with frizzled grey hair. Her body was shapeless in a wrapper and her feet slithered in loose slippers. A man with a polished bald head and milky eyes sat in a wicker chair beside a table. He held his hands in his lap and twisted the knuckles aimlessly. He didn't look towards the door.

Steve said: 'I'm from Miss Chiozza. Are you Agatha's mother?'

The woman said dully: 'I reckon. But she ain't home, mister.' The man in the chair got a handkerchief from somewhere and blew his nose. He snickered darkly.

Steve said: 'Miss Chiozza's not feeling so well tonight. She was hoping Agatha would come back and stay the night with her.'

The milky-eyed man snickered again, sharply. The woman

said: 'We dunno where she is. She don't come home. Pa'n me waits up for her to come home. She stays out till we're sick.'

The old man snapped in a reedy voice: 'She'll stay out till the cops get her one of these times.'

'Pa's half blind,' the woman said. 'Makes him kinda mean. Won't you step in?'

Steve shook his head and turned his hat around in his hands like a bashful cowpuncher in a horse opera. 'I've got to find her,' he said. 'Where would she go?'

'Out drinkin' liquor with cheap spenders,' Pa cackled. 'Panty-waists with silk handkerchiefs 'stead of neckties. If I had eyes, I'd strap her till she dropped.' He grabbed the arms of his chair and the muscles knotted on the backs of his hands. Then he began to cry. Tears welled from his milky eyes and started through the white stubble on his cheeks. The woman went across and took the handkerchief out of his fist and wiped his face with it. Then she blew her nose on it and came back to the door.

'Might be anywhere,' she said to Steve. 'This is a big town, mister. I dunno where at to say.'

Steve said dully: 'I'll call back. If she comes in, will you hang on to her. What's your phone number?'

'What's the phone number, Pa?' the woman called back over her shoulder.

'I ain't sayin',' Pa snorted.

The woman said: 'I remember now. South Two-four-five-four. Call anytime. Pa'n me ain't got nothing to do.'

Steve thanked her and went back down the white walk to the street and along the walk half a block to where he had left his car. He glanced idly across the way and started to get into his car, then stopped moving suddenly with his hand gripping the car door. He let go of that, took three steps sideways and stood looking across the street tight-mouthed.

All the houses in the block were much the same, but the one opposite had a FOR RENT placard stuck in the front window and a real-estate sign spiked into the small patch of front lawn. The house itself looked neglected, utterly empty, but in its little driveway stood a small neat black coupé.

Steve said under his breath: 'Hunch. Play it up, Stevie.'

He walked almost delicately across the wide dusty street, his hand touching the hard metal of the gun in his pocket, and came up behind the little car, stood and listened. He moved silently along its left side, glanced back across the street, then looked in the car's open left-front window.

The girl sat almost as if driving, except that her head was tipped a little too much into the corner. The little red hat was still on her head, the grey coat, trimmed with fur, still around her body. In the reflected moonlight her mouth was strained open. Her tongue stuck out. And her chestnut eyes stared at the roof of the car.

Steve didn't touch her. He didn't have to touch her or look any closer to know there would be heavy bruises on her neck.

'Tough on women, these guys,' he muttered.

The girl's big black brocade bag lay on the seat beside her, gaping open like her mouth – like Miss Marilyn Delorme's mouth, and Miss Marilyn Delorme's purple bag.

'Yeah – tough on women.'

He backed away till he stood under a small palm tree by the entrance to the driveway. The street was as empty and deserted as a closed theatre. He crossed silently to his car, got into it and drove away.

Nothing to it. A girl coming home alone late at night, stuck up and strangled a few doors from her own home by some tough guy. Very simple. The first prowl car that cruised that block – if the boys were half awake – would take a look the minute they spotted the FOR RENT sign. Steve tramped hard on the throttle and went away from there.

At Washington and Figueroa he went into an all-night drugstore and pulled shut the door of the phone booth at the back. He dropped his nickel and dialled the number of police headquarters.

He asked for the desk and said: 'Write this down, will you,

sergeant? Brighton Avenue, thirty-two-hundred block, west side, in driveway of empty house. Got that much?'

'Yeah. So what?'

'Car with dead woman in it,' Steve said, and hung up.

Seven

Quillan, head day clerk and assistant manager of the Carlton Hotel, was on night duty, because Millar, the night auditor, was off for a week. It was half-past one and things were dead and Quillan was bored. He had done everything there was to do long ago, because he had been an hotel man for twenty years and there was nothing to it.

The night porter had finished cleaning up and was in his room beside the elevator bank. One elevator was lighted and open, as usual. The main lobby had been tidied up and the lights had been properly dimmed. Everything was exactly as usual.

Quillan was a rather short, rather thickset man with clear bright toadlike eyes that seemed to hold a friendly expression without really having any expression at all. He had pale sandy hair and not much of it. His pale hands were clasped in front of him on the marble top of the desk. He was just the right height to put his weight on the desk without looking as if he were sprawling. He was looking at the wall across the entrance lobby, but he wasn't seeing it. He was half asleep, even though his eyes were wide open, and if the night porter struck a match behind his door, Quillan would know it and bang on his bell.

The brass-trimmed swing doors at the street entrance pushed open and Steve Grayce came in, a summer-weight coat turned up around his neck, his hat yanked low and a cigarette wisping smoke at the corner of his mouth. He looked very casual, very alert, and very much at ease. He strolled over to the desk and rapped on it.

'Wake up!' he snorted.

Quillan moved his eyes an inch and said: 'All outside rooms with bath. But positively no parties on the eighth floor. Hiyah, Steve. So you finally got the axe. And for the wrong thing. That's life.'

Steve said: 'Okay. Have you got a new night man here?'

'Don't need one, Steve. Never did, in my opinion.'

'You'll need one as long as old hotel men like you register floozies on the same corridor with people like Leopardi.'

Quillan half closed his eyes and then opened them to where they had been before. He said indifferently: 'Not me, pal. But anybody can make a mistake. Millar's really an accountant – not a desk man.'

Steve leaned back and his face became very still. The smoke almost hung at the tip of his cigarette. His eyes were like black glass now. He smiled a little dishonestly.

'And why was Leopardi put in a four-dollar room on Eight instead of in a tower suite at twenty-eight per?'

Quillan smiled back at him. 'I didn't register Leopardi, old sock. There were reservations in. I supposed they were what he wanted. Some guys don't spend. Any other questions, Mr Grayce?'

'Yeah. Was eight-fourteen empty last night?'

'It was on change, so it was empty. Something about the plumbing. Proceed.'

'Who marked it on change?'

Quillan's bright fathomless eyes turned and became curiously fixed. He didn't answer.

Steve said: 'Here's why. Leopardi was in eight-fifteen and the two girls in eight-eleven. Just eight-thirteen between. A lad with a pass-key could have gone into eight-thirteen and turned both the bolt locks on the communicating doors. Then, if the folks in the two other rooms had done the same thing on their side, they'd have a suite set up.'

'So what?' Quillan asked. 'We got chiselled out of eight bucks, eh? Well, it happens, in better hotels than this.' His eyes looked sleepy now.

Steve said: 'Millar could have done that. But hell, it doesn't make sense. Millar's not that kind of a guy. Risk a job for a buck tip – phooey. Millar's no dollar pimp.'

Quillan said: 'All right, policeman. Tell me what's really on your mind.'

'One of the girls in eight-eleven had a gun. Leopardi got a threat letter yesterday – I don't know where or how. It didn't faze him, though. He tore it up. That's how I know. I collected the pieces from his basket. I suppose Leopardi's boys all checked out of here.'

'Of course. They went to the Normandy.'

'Call the Normandy, and ask to speak to Leopardi. If he's there, he'll still be at the bottle. Probably with a gang.'

'Why?' Quilland asked gently.

'Because you're a nice guy. If Leopardi answers – just hang up.' Steve paused and pinched his chin hard. 'If he went out, try to find out where.'

Quillan straightened, gave Steve another long quiet look and went behind the pebbled-glass screen. Steve stood very still, listening, one hand clenched at his side, the other tapping noiselessly on the marble desk.

In about three minutes Quillan came back and leaned on the desk again and said: 'Not there. Party going on in his suite – they sold him a big one – and sounds loud. I talked to a guy who was fairly sober. He said Leopardi got a call around ten – some girl. He went out preening himself, as the fellow says. Hinting about a very juicy date. The guy was just lit enough to hand me all this.'

Steve said: 'You're a real pal. I hate not to tell you the rest. Well, I liked working here. Not much work at that.'

He started towards the entrance doors again. Quillan let him get his hand on the brass handle before he called out. Steve turned and came back slowly.

Quillan said: 'I heard Leopardi took a shot at you. I don't

think it was noticed. It wasn't reported down here. And I don't think Peters fully realized that until he saw the mirror in eight-fifteen. If you care to come back, Steve—'

Steve shook his head. 'Thanks for the thought.'

'And hearing about that shot,' Quillan added, 'made me remember something. Two years ago a girl shot herself in eight-fifteen.'

Steve straightened his back so sharply that he almost jumped. 'What girl?'

Quillan looked surprised. 'I don't know. I don't remember her real name. Some girl who had been kicked around all she could stand and wanted to die in a clean bed – alone.'

Steve reached across and took hold of Quillan's arm. 'The hotel files,' he rasped. 'The clippings, whatever there was in the papers will be in them. I want to see those clippings.'

Quillan stared at him for a long moment. Then he said: 'Whatever game you're playing, kid – you're playing it damn close to your vest. I will say that for you. And me bored stiff with a night to kill.'

He reached along the desk and thumped the call bell. The door of the night porter's room opened and the porter came across the entrance lobby. He nodded and smiled at Steve.

Quillan said: 'Take the board, Carl. I'll be in Mr Peters' office for a little while.'

He went to the safe and got keys out of it.

Eight

The cabin was high up on the side of the mountain, against a thick growth of digger pine, oak and incense cedar. It was solidly built, with a stone chimney, shingled all over and heavily braced against the slope of the hill. By daylight the roof was green and the sides dark reddish brown and the window frames and draw curtains red. In the uncanny brightness of an all-night mid-October moon in the mountains, it stood out sharply in every detail, except colour.

It was at the end of a road, a quarter of a mile from any other cabin. Steve rounded the bend towards it without lights at five in the morning. He stopped his car at once, when he was sure it was the right cabin, got out and walked soundlessly along the side of the gravel road, on a carpet of wild iris.

On the road level there was a rough pine board garage, and from this a path went up to the cabin porch. The garage was unlocked. Steve swung the door open carefully, groped in past the dark bulk of a car and felt the top of the radiator. It was still warmish. He got a small flash out of his pocket and played it over the car. A grey sedan, dusty, the gas gauge low. He snapped the flash off, shut the garage door carefully and slipped into place the piece of wood that served for a hasp. Then he climbed the path to the house.

There was light behind the drawn red curtains. The porch was high and juniper logs were piled on it, with the bark still on them. The front door had a thumb latch and a rustic door handle above.

He went up, neither too softly nor too noisily, lifted his hand, sighed deep in his throat, and knocked. His hand touched the butt of the gun in the inside pocket of his coat, once, then came away empty.

A chair creaked and steps padded across the floor and a voice called out softly: 'What is it?' Millar's voice.

Steve put his lips close to the wood and said: 'This is Steve, George. You up already?'

The key turned, and the door opened. George Millar, the dapper night auditor of the Carlton House, didn't look dapper now. He was dressed in old trousers and a thick blue sweater with a roll collar. His feet were in ribbed wool socks and fleece-lined slippers. His clipped black moustache was a curved smudge across his pale face. Two electric bulbs burned in their sockets in a low beam across the room, below the slope of the high roof. A table lamp was lit and its shade was tilted to throw light on a big Morris chair with a leather seat and back-cushion. A fire burned lazily in a heap of soft ash on the big open hearth.

Millar said in his low, husky voice: 'Hell's sake, Steve. Glad to see you. How'd you find us anyway? Come on in, guy.'

Steve stepped through the door and Millar locked it. 'City habit,' he said grinning. 'Nobody locks anything in the mountains. Have a chair. Warm your toes. Cold out at this time of night.'

Steve said: 'Yeah. Plenty cold.'

He sat down in the Morris chair and put his hat and coat on the end of the solid wood table behind it. He leaned forward and held his hands out to the fire.

Millar said: 'How the hell did you find us, Steve?'

Steve didn't look at him. He said quietly: 'Not so easy at that. You told me last night your brother had a cabin up here – remember? So I had nothing to do, so I thought I'd drive up and bum some breakfast. The guy in the inn at Crestline didn't know who had cabins where. His trade is with people passing through. I rang up a garage man and he didn't know any Millar cabin. Then I saw a light come on down the street in a coal-and-wood yard and a little guy who is forest ranger and deputy sheriff and wood-and-gas dealer and half a dozen other things was getting his car out to go down to San Bernardino for some tank gas. A very smart little guy. The minute I said your brother had been a fighter he wised up. So here I am.'

Millar pawed at his moustache. Bedsprings creaked at the back of the cabin somewhere. 'Sure, he still goes under his fighting name – Gaff Talley. I'll get him up and we'll have some coffee. I guess you and me are both in the same boat. Used to working at night and can't sleep. I haven't been to bed at all.'

Steve looked at him slowly and looked away. A burly voice behind them said: 'Gaff is up. Who's your pal, George?'

Steve stood up casually and turned. He looked at the man's

hands first. He couldn't help himself. They were large hands, well kept as to cleanliness, but coarse and ugly. One knuckle had been broken badly. He was a big man with reddish hair. He wore a sloppy bathrobe over outing-flannel pyjamas. He had a leathery expressionless face, scarred over the cheekbones. There were fine white scars over his eyebrows and at the corners of his mouth. His nose was spread and thick. His whole face looked as if it had caught a lot of gloves. His eyes alone looked vaguely like Millar's eyes.

Millar said: 'Steve Grayce. Night man at the hotel – until last night.' His grin was a little vague.

Gaff Talley came over and shook hands. 'Glad to meet you,' he said. 'I'll get some duds on and we'll scrape a breakfast off the shelves. I slept enough. George ain't slept any, the poor sap.'

He went back across the room towards the door through which he'd come. He stopped there and leaned on an old phonograph, put his big hand down behind a pile of records in paper envelopes. He stayed just like that, without moving.

Millar said: 'Any luck on a job, Steve? Or did you try yet?'

'Yeah. In a way. I guess I'm a sap, but I'm going to have a shot at the private-agency racket. Not much in it unless I can land some publicity.' He shrugged. Then he said very quietly: 'King Leopardi's been bumped off.'

Millar's mouth snapped wide open. He stayed like that for almost a minute – perfectly still, with his mouth open. Gaff Talley leaned against the wall and stared without showing anything in his face. Millar finally said: 'Bumped off? Where? Don't tell me—'

'Not in the hotel, George. Too bad, wasn't it? In a girl's apartment. Nice girl too. She didn't entice him there. The old suicide gag – only it won't work. And the girl is my client.'

Millar didn't move. Neither did the big man. Steve leaned his shoulders against the stone mantel. He said softly: 'I went out to the Club Shalotte this afternoon to apologize to Leopardi. Silly idea, because I didn't owe him an apology. There was a girl there in the bar lounge with him. He took three socks at me and left. The girl didn't like that. We got rather clubby. Had a drink together. Then late tonight – last night – she called me up and said Leopardi was over at her place and he was drunk and she couldn't get rid of him. I went there. Only he wasn't drunk. He was dead, in her bed, in yellow pyjamas.'

The big man lifted his left hand and roughed back his hair. Millar leaned slowly against the edge of the table, as if he were afraid the edge might be sharp enough to cut him. His mouth twitched under the clipped back moustache.

He said huskily: 'That's lousy.'

The big man said: 'Well, for cyin' into a milk bottle.'

Steve said: 'Only they weren't Leopardi's pyjamas. His had initials on them – big black initials. And his were satin, not silk. And although he had a gun in his hand – this girl's gun by the way – *he* didn't shoot himself in the heart. The cops will determine that. Maybe you birds never heard of the Lund test, with paraffin wax, to find out who did or didn't fire a gun recently. The kill ought to have been pulled in the hotel last night, in room eight-fifteen. I spoiled that by heaving him out on his neck before that black-haired girl in eight-eleven could get to him. Didn't I, George?'

Millar said: 'I guess you did – if I know what you're talking about.'

Steve said slowly: 'I think you know what I'm talking about, George. It would have been a kind of poetic justice if King Leopardi had been knocked off in room eight-fifteen. Because that was the room where a girl shot herself two years ago. A girl who registered as Mary Smith – but whose usual name was Eve Talley. And whose real name was Eve Millar.'

The big man leaned heavily on the victrola and said thickly: 'Maybe I ain't woke up yet. That sounds like it might grow up to be a dirty crack. We had a sister named Eve that shot herself in the Carlton. So what?'

Steve smiled a little crookedly. He said: 'Listen, George. You told me Quillan registered those girls in eight-eleven. *You* did. You told me Leopardi registered on Eight, instead of in a good suite, because he was tight. He wasn't tight. He just didn't care where he was put, as long as female company was handy. And you saw to that. You planned the whole thing, George. You even got Peters to write Leopardi at the Raleigh in 'Frisco and ask him to use the Carlton when he came down – because the same man owned it who owned the Club Shalotte. As if a guy like Jumbo Walters would care where a bandleader registered.'

Millar's face was dead white, expressionless. His voice cracked. 'Steve – for God's sake, Steve, what are you talking about? How the hell could I—'

'Sorry, kid. I liked working with you. I liked you a lot. I guess I still like you. But I don't like people who strangle women – or people who smear women in order to cover up a revenge murder.'

His hand shot up – and stopped. The big man said: 'Take it easy – and look at this one.'

Gaff's hand had come up from behind the pile of records. A Colt .45 was in it. He said between his teeth: 'I always thought house dicks were just a bunch of cheap grafters. I guess I missed out on you. You got a few brains. Hell, I bet you even run out to One-eighteen Court Street. Right?'

Steve let his hand fall empty and looked straight at the big Colt. 'Right. I saw the girl – dead – with your fingers marked into her neck. They can measure those, fella. Killing Dolores Chiozza's maid the same way was a mistake. They'll match up the two sets of marks, find out that your black-haired gun girl was at the Carlton last night, and piece the whole story together. With the information they get at the hotel they can't miss. I give you two weeks, if you beat it quick. And I mean quick.'

Millar licked his dry lips and said softly: 'There's no hurry, Steve. No hurry at all. Our job is done. Maybe not the best way, maybe not the nicest way, but it wasn't a nice job. And Leopardi was the worst kind of a louse. We loved our sister, and he made a tramp out of her. She was a wide-eyed kid that fell for a flashy greaseball, and the greaseball went up in the world and threw her out on her ear for a red-headed torcher who was more his kind. He threw her out and broke her heart and she killed herself.'

Steve said harshly: 'Yeah – and what were you doing all that time – manicuring your nails?'

'We weren't around when it happened. It took us a little time to find out the why of it.'

Steve said: 'So that was worth killing four people for, was it? And as for Dolorés Chiozza, she wouldn't have wiped her feet on Leopardi – then, or any time since. But you had to put her in the middle too, with your rotten little revenge murder. You make me sick, George. Tell your big tough brother to get on with his murder party.'

The big man grinned and said: 'Nuff talk, George. See has he a gat – and don't get behind him or in front of him. This beanshooter goes on through.'

Steve stared at the big man's .45. His face was hard as white bone. There was a thin cold sneer on his lips and his eyes were cold and dark.

Millar moved softly in his fleece-lined slippers. He came around the end of the table and went close to Steve's side and reached out a hand to tap his pockets. He stepped back and pointed: 'In there.'

Steve said softly: 'I must be nuts. I could have taken you then, George.'

Gaff Talley barked: 'Stand away from him.'

He walked solidly across the room and put the big Colt against Steve's stomach hard. He reached up with his left hand and worked the Detective Special from the inside breast pocket. His eyes were sharp on Steve's eyes. He held Steve's gun out behind him. 'Take this, George.'

Millar took the gun and went over beyond the big table again and stood at the far corner of it. Gaff Talley backed away from Steve.

'You're through, wise guy,' he said. 'You got to know that. There's only two ways outa these mountains and we gotta have time. And maybe you didn't tell nobody. See?'

Steve stood like a rock, his face white, a twisted half-smile working at the corners of his lips. He stared hard at the big man's gun and his stare was faintly puzzled.

Millar said: 'Does it have to be that way, Gaff?' His voice was a croak now, without tone, without its usual pleasant huskiness.

Steve turned his head a little and looked at Millar. 'Sure it has, George. You're just a couple of cheap hoodlums after all. A couple of nasty-minded sadists playing at being avengers of wronged girlhood. Hillbilly stuff. And right this minute you're practically cold meat – cold, rotten meat.'

Gaff Talley laughed and cocked the big revolver with his thumb. 'Say your prayers, guy,' he jeered.

Steve said grimly: 'What makes you think you're going to bump me off with that thing? No shells in it, strangler. Better try to take me the way you handle women – with your hands.'

The big man's eyes flicked down, clouded. Then he roared with laughter. 'Geez, the dust on that one must be a foot thick,' he chuckled. 'Watch.'

He pointed the big gun at the floor and squeezed the trigger. The firing pin clicked dryly – on an empty chamber. The big man's face convulsed.

For a short moment nobody moved. Then Gaff turned slowly on the balls of his feet and looked at his brother. He said almost gently: 'You, George?'

Millar licked his lips and gulped. He had to move his mouth in and out before he could speak.

'Me, Gaff. I was standing by the window when Steve got out of his car down the road, I saw him go into the garage. I knew the car would still be warm. There's been enough killing, Gaff. Too much. So I took the shells out of your gun.'

Millar's thumb moved back the hammer on the Detective Special. Gaff's eyes bulged. He stared fascinated at the snub-nosed gun. Then he lunged violently towards it, flailing with the empty Colt. Millar braced himself and stood very still and said dimly, like an old man: 'Good-bye, Gaff.'

The gun jumped three times in his small neat hand. Smoke

curled lazily from its muzzle. A piece of burned log fell over in the fireplace.

Gaff Talley smiled queerly and stooped and stood perfectly still. The gun dropped at his feet. He put his big heavy hands against his stomach, said slowly, thickly: ' 'S all right, kid. 'S all right, I guess . . . I guess I . . .'

His voice trailed off and his legs began to twist under him. Steve took three long quick silent steps, and slammed Millar hard on the angle of the jaw. The big man was still falling – as slowly as a tree falls.

Millar spun across the room and crashed against the end wall and a blue-and-white plate fell off the plate-moulding and broke. The gun sailed from his fingers. Steve dived for it and came up with it. Millar crouched and watched his brother.

Gaff Talley bent his head to the floor and braced his hands and then lay down quietly, on his stomach, like a man who was very tired. He made no sound of any kind.

Daylight showed at the windows, around the red glass-curtains. The piece of broken log smoked against the side of the hearth and the rest of the fire was a heap of soft grey ash with a glow at its heart.

Steve said dully: 'You saved my life, George – or at least you saved a lot of shooting. I took the chance because what I wanted was evidence. Step over there to the desk and write it all out and sign it.'

Millar said: 'Is he dead?'

'He's dead, George. You killed him. Write that too.'

Millar said quietly: 'It's funny. I wanted to finish Leopardi myself, with my own hands, when he was at the top, when he had the farthest to fall. Just finish him and then take what came. But Gaff was the guy who wanted it done cute. Gaff, the tough mug who never had any education and never dodged a punch in his life, wanted to do it smart and figure angles. Well, maybe that's why he owned property, like that apartment house on Court Street that Jake Stoyanoff managed for him. I don't know how he got to Dolores Chiozza's maid. It doesn't matter much, does it?'

Steve said: 'Go and write it. You were the one called Leopardi up and pretended to be the girl, huh?'

Millar said: 'Yes. I'll write it all down, Steve. I'll sign it and then you'll let me go – just for an hour. Won't you, Steve? Just an hour's start. That's not much to ask of an old friend, is it, Steve?'

Millar smiled. It was a small, frail, ghostly smile. Steve bent beside the big sprawled man and felt his neck artery. He looked up, said: 'Quite dead . . . Yes, you get an hour's start, George – if you write it all out.'

Millar walked softly over to a tall oak highboy desk, studded with tarnished brass nails. He opened the flap and sat down and reached for a pen. He unscrewed the top from a bottle of ink and began to write in his neat, clear accountant's handwriting.

Steve Grayce sat down in front of the fire and lit a cigarette and stared at the ashes. He held the gun with his left hand on his knee. Outside the cabin, birds began to sing. Inside there was no sound but the scratching pen.

Nine

The sun was well up when Steve left the cabin, locked it up, walked down the steep path and along the narrow gravel road to his car. The garage was empty now. The grey sedan was gone. Smoke from another cabin floated lazily above the pines and oaks half a mile away. He started his car, drove it around a bend, past two old boxcars that had been converted into cabins, then on to a main road with a stripe down the middle and so up the hill to Crestline.

He parked on the main street before the Rim-of-the-World Inn, had a cup of coffee at the counter, then shut himself in a phone booth at the back of the empty lounge. He had the long distance operator get Jumbo Walters' number in Los Angeles, then called the owner of the Club Shalotte.

A voice said silkily: 'This is Mr Walters' residence.'

'Steve Grayce. Put him on, if you please.'

'One moment, please.' A click, another voice, not so smooth and much harder. 'Yeah?'

'Steve Grayce. I want to speak to Mr Walters.'

'Sorry. I don't seem to know you. It's a little early, amigo. What's your business?'

'Did he go to Miss Chiozza's place?'

'Oh.' A pause. 'The shamus. I get it. Hold the line, pal.'

Another voice now – lazy, with the faintest colour of Irish in it. 'You can talk, son. This is Walters.'

'I'm Steve Grayce. I'm the man—'

'I know all about that, son. The lady is okay, by the way. I think she's asleep upstairs. Go on.'

'I'm at Crestline – top of the Arrowhead grade. Two men murdered Leopardi. One was George Millar, night auditor at the Carlton Hotel. The other his brother, an ex-fighter named Gaff Talley. Talley's dead – shot by his brother. Millar got away – but he left me a full confession signed, detailed, complete.'

Walters said slowly: 'You're a fast worker, son – unless you're just plain crazy. Better come in here fast. Why did they do it?'

'They had a sister.'

Walters repeated quietly: 'They had a sister . . . What about this fellow that got away? We don't want some hick sheriff or publicity-hungry county attorney to get ideas—'

Steve broke in quietly: 'I don't think you'll have to worry about that, Mr Walters. I think I know where he's gone.'

He ate breakfast at the inn, not because he was hungry, but because he was weak. He got into his car again and started down the long smooth grade from Crestline to San Bernardino, a broad paved boulevard skirting the edge of a sheer drop into the deep valley. There were places where the road went close to the edge, white guard-fences alongside.

Two miles below Crestline was the place. The road made a sharp turn around a shoulder of the mountain. Cars were parked on the gravel off the pavement – several private cars, an official car, and a wrecking car. The white fence was broken through and men stood around the broken place looking down.

Eight hundred feet below, what was left of a grey sedan lay silent and crumpled in the morning sunshine.

The Simple Art of Murder

Fiction in any form has always intended to be realistic. Old-fashioned novels which now seem stilted and artificial to the point of burlesque did not appear that way to the people who first read them. Writers like Fielding and Smollett could seem realistic in the modern sense because they dealt largely with uninhibited characters, many of whom were about two jumps ahead of the police, but Jane Austen's chronicles of highly inhibited people against a background of rural gentility seem real enough psychologically. There is plenty of that kind of social and emotional hypocrisy around today. Add to it a liberal dose of intellectual pretentiousness and you get the tone of the book page in your daily paper and the earnest and fatuous atmosphere breathed by discussion groups in little clubs. These are the people who make best-sellers, which are promotional jobs based on a sort of indirect snob-appeal, carefully escorted by the trained seals of the critical fraternity, and lovingly tended and watered by certain much too powerful pressure groups whose business is selling books, although they would like you to think they are fostering culture. Just get a little behind in your payments and you will find out how idealistic they are.

The detective story for a variety of reasons can seldom be promoted. It is usually about murder and hence lacks the element of uplift. Murder, which is a frustration of the individual and hence a frustration of the race, may have, and in fact has, a good deal of sociological implication. But it has been going on too long for it to be news. If the mystery novel is at all realistic (which it very seldom is) it is written in a certain spirit of detachment; otherwise nobody but a psychopath would want to write it or read it. The murder novel has also a depressing way of minding its own business, solving its own problems and answering its own questions. There is nothing left to discuss, except whether it was well enough written to be good fiction, and the people who make up the half-million sales wouldn't know that anyway. The detection of quality in writing is difficult enough even for those who make a career of the job, without paying too much attention to the matter of advance sales.

The detective story (perhaps I had better call it that, since the English formula still dominates the trade) has to find its public by a slow process of distillation. That it does do this, and holds on thereafter with such tenacity, is a fact; the reasons for it are a study for more patient minds than mine. Nor is it any part of my thesis to maintain that it is a vital and significant form of art. There are no vital and significant forms of art; there is only art, and precious little of that. The growth of populations has in no way increased the amount; it has merely increased the adeptness with which substitutes can be produced and packaged.

Yet the detective story, even in its most conventional form, is difficult to write well. Good specimens of the art are much rarer than good serious novels. Rather second-rate items outlast most of the high velocity fiction, and a great many that should never have been born simply refuse to die at all. They are as durable as the statues in public parks and just about that dull.

This is very annoying to people of what is called discernment. They do not like it that penetrating and important works of fiction of a few years back stand on their special shelf in the library marked 'Best-sellers of Yesteryear', and nobody goes near them but an occasional shortsighted customer who bends down, peers briefly and hurries away; while old ladies jostle each other at the mystery shelf to grab off some item of the same vintage with a title like *The Triple Murder Case*, or *Inspector Pinchbottle to the Rescue*. They do not like it that 'really important books' get dusty on the reprint counter, while *Death Wears Yellow Garters* is put out in editions of fifty or one hundred thousand copies on the news-stands of the country, and is obviously not there just to say good-bye.

To tell you the truth, I do not like it very much myself. In my less stilted moments I too write detective stories, and all this immortality makes just a little too much competition. Even Einstein couldn't get very far if three hundred treatises of the high physics were published every year, and several thousand others in some form or other were hanging around in excellent condition, and being read too.

Hemingway says somewhere that the good writer competes only with the dead. The good detective story writer (there must after all be a few) competes not only with all the unburied dead but with all the hosts of the living as well. And on almost equal terms; for it is one of the qualities of this kind of writing that the thing that makes people read it never goes out of style. The hero's tie may be a little off the mode and the good grey inspector may arrive in a dogcart instead of a streamlined sedan with siren screaming, but what he does when he gets there is the same old fussing around with timetables and bits of charred paper and who trampled the jolly old flowering arbutus under the library window.

I have, however, a less sordid interest in the matter. It seems to me that production of detective stories on so large a scale, and by writers whose immediate reward is small and whose need of critical praise is almost nil would not be possible at all if the job took any talent. In that sense the raised eyebrow of the critic and the shoddy merchandising of the publisher are perfectly logical. The average detective story is probably no worse than the average novel, but you never see the average novel. It doesn't get published. The average – or only slightly above average – detective story does. Not only is it published but it is sold in small quantities to rental libraries, and it is read. There are even a few optimists who buy it at the full retail price of two dollars, because it looks so fresh and new, and there is a picture of a corpse on the cover.

And the strange thing is that this average, more than

middling dull pooped-out piece of utterly unreal and mechanical fiction is not terribly different from what are called the masterpieces of the art. It drags on a little more slowly, the dialogue is a little greyer, the cardboard out of which the characters are cut is a shade thinner, and the cheating is a little more obvious; but it is the same kind of book. Whereas the good novel is not at all the same kind of book as the bad novel. It is about entirely different things. But the good detective story and the bad detective story are about exactly the same things, and they are about them in very much the same way. (There are reasons for this too, and reasons for the reasons; there always are.)

I suppose the principal dilemma of the traditional or classic or straight-deductive or logic-and-deduction novel of detection is that for any approach to perfection it demands a combination of qualities not found in the same mind. The cool-headed constructionist does not also come across with lively characters, sharp dialogue, a sense of pace and an acute use of observed detail. The grim logician has as much atmosphere as a drawing-board. The scientific sleuth has a nice new shiny laboratory, but I'm sorry I can't remember the face. The fellow who can write you a vivid and colourful prose simply won't be bothered with the coolie labour of breaking down unbreakable alibis.

The master of rare knowledge is living psychologically in the age of the hoop skirt. If you know all you should know about ceramics and Egyptian needlework, you don't know anything at all about the police. If you know that platinum won't melt under about 2,800 degrees Fahrenheit by itself, but will melt at the glance of a pair of deep blue eyes when put close to a bar of lead, then you don't know how men make love in the twentieth century. And if you know enough about the elegant flânerie of the pre-war French Riviera to lay your story in that locale, you don't know that a couple of capsules of barbital small enough to be swallowed will not only not kill a man – they will not even put him to sleep if he fights against them.

Every detective story writer makes mistakes, and none will ever know as much as he should. Conan Doyle made mistakes which completely invalidated some of his stories, but he was a pioneer, and Sherlock Holmes after all is mostly an attitude and a few dozen lines of unforgettable dialogue. It is the ladies and gentlemen of what Mr Howard Haycraft (in his book *Murder for Pleasure*) calls the Golden Age of detective fiction that really get me down. This age is not remote. For Mr Haycraft's purpose it starts after the First World War and lasts up to about 1930. For all practical purposes it is still here. Two-thirds or three-quarters of all the detective stories published still adhere to the formula the giants of this era created, perfected, polished and sold to the world as problems in logic and deduction.

These are stern words, but be not alarmed. They are only words. Let us glance at one of the glories of the literature, an acknowledged masterpiece of the art of fooling the reader without cheating him. It is called *The Red House Mystery*, was written by A. A. Milne, and has been named by Alexander Woollcott (rather a fast man with a superlative) 'One of the three best mystery stories of all time.' Words of that size are not spoken lightly. The book was published in 1922, but is quite timeless, and might as easily have been published in July 1939, or, with a few slight changes, last week. It ran thirteen editions and seems to have been in print, in the original format, for about sixteen years. That happens to few books of any kind. It is an agreeable book, light, amusing in the *Punch* style, written with a deceptive smoothness that is not so easy as it looks.

It concerns Mark Ablett's impersonation of his brother Robert, as a hoax on his friends. Mark is the owner of the Red House, a typical laburnum and lodge gate English country house, and he has a secretary who encourages him and abets him in this impersonation, because the secretary is going to murder him, if he pulls it off. Nobody around the Red House has ever seen Robert, fifteen years absent in Australia, known to them by repute as a no-good. A letter from Robert is talked about, but never shown. It announces his arrival, and Mark hints it will not be a pleasant occasion. One afternoon, then, the supposed Robert arrives, identifies himself to a couple of servants, is shown into the study, and Mark (according to testimony at the inquest) goes in after him. Robert is then found dead on the floor with a bullet-hole in his face, and of course Mark has vanished into thin air. Arrive the police, suspect Mark must be the murderer, remove the debris and proceed with the investigation, and in due course, with the inquest.

Milne is aware of one very difficult hurdle and tries as well as he can to get over it. Since the secretary is going to murder Mark once he has established himself as Robert, the impersonation has to continue on and fool the police. Since, also, everybody around the Red House knows Mark intimately, disguise is necessary. This is achieved by shaving off Mark's beard, roughening his hands ('not the manicured hands of a gentleman' – testimony) and the use of a gruff voice and rough manner.

But this is not enough. The cops are going to have the body and the clothes on it and whatever is in the pockets. Therefore none of this must suggest Mark. Milne therefore works like a switch engine to put over the motivation that Mark is such a thoroughly conceited performer that he dresses the part down to the socks and underwear (from all of which the secretary has removed the maker's labels), like a ham blacking himself all over to play Othello. If the reader will buy this (and the sales record shows he must have) Milne figures he is solid. Yet, however light in texture the story may be, it is offered as a problem of logic and deduction.

If it is not that, it is nothing at all. There is nothing else for it to be. If the situation is false, you cannot even accept it as a light novel, for there is no story for the light novel to be about. If the problem does not contain the elements of truth and plausibility, it is no problem; if the logic is an illusion, there is nothing to deduce. If the impersonation is impossible once the reader is told the conditions it must fulfil, then the whole thing is a fraud. Not a deliberate fraud, because Milne would not have written the story, if he had known what he was up against. He is up against a number of deadly things, none of which he even considers. Nor, apparently, does the casual reader, who wants to like the story, hence takes it at its face value. But the reader is not called upon to know the facts of life; it is the author who is the expert in the case. Here is what this author ignores:

1 The coroner holds formal jury inquest on a body for which no legally competent identification is offered. A coroner, usually in a big city, will sometimes hold inquest on a body that *cannot* be identified, if the record of such an inquest has or may have a value (fire, disaster, evidence of murder, etc.). No such reason exists here, and there is no one to identify the body. A couple of witnesses said the man said he was Robert Ablett. This is mere presumption, and has weight only if nothing conflicts with it. Identification is a condition precedent to an inquest. Even in death a man has a right to his own identity. The coroner will, wherever humanly possible, enforce that right. To neglect it would be a violation of his office.

2 Since Mark Ablett, missing and suspected of the murder, cannot defend himself, all evidence of his movements before and after the murder is vital (as also whether he has money to run away on); yet all such evidence is given by the man closest to the murder, and is without corroboration. It is automatically suspect until proved true.

3 The police find by direct investigation that Robert Ablett was not well thought of in his native village. Somebody there must have known him. No such person was brought to the inquest. (The story couldn't stand it.)

4 The police know there is an element of threat in Robert's supposed visit, and that it is connected with the murder must be obvious to them. Yet they make no attempt to check Robert in Australia, or find out what character he had there, or what associates, or even if he actually came to England,

and with whom. (If they had, they would have found out he had been dead three years.)

5 The police surgeon examines the body, with a recently shaved beard (exposing unweathered skin), artificially roughened hands, yet the body of a wealthy, soft-living man, long resident in a cool climate. Robert was a rough individual and had lived fifteen years in Australia. That is the surgeon's information. It is impossible he would have noticed nothing to conflict with it.

6 The clothes are nameless, empty, and have had the labels removed. Yet the man wearing them asserted an identity. The presumption that he was not what he said he was is overpowering. Nothing whatever is done about this peculiar circumstance. It is never even mentioned as being peculiar.

7 A man is missing, a well-known local man, and a body in the morgue closely resembles him. It is impossible that the police should not at once eliminate the chance that the missing man *is* the dead man. Nothing would be easier than to prove it. Not even to think of it is incredible. It makes idiots of the police, so that a brash amateur may startle the world with a fake solution.

The detective in the case is an insouciant amateur named Anthony Gillingham, a nice lad with a cheery eye, a cosy little flat in London, and that airy manner. He is not making any money on the assignment, but is always available when the local *gendarmerie* loses its notebook. The English police seem to endure him with their customary stoicism; but I shudder to think of what the boys down at the Homicide Bureau in my city would do to him.

There are less plausible examples of the art than this. In *Trent's Last Case* (often called 'the perfect detective story') you have to accept the premiss that a grant of international finance, whose lightest frown makes Wall Street quiver like a chihuahua, will plot his own death so as to hang his secretary, and that the secretary when pinched will maintain an aristocratic silence; the old Etonian in him maybe. I have known relatively few international financiers, but I rather think the author of this novel has (if possible) known fewer.

There is one by Freeman Wills Crofts (the soundest builder of them all when he doesn't get too fancy) wherein a murderer by the aid of make-up, split-second timing, and some very sweet evasive action, impersonates the man he has just killed and thereby gets him alive and distant from the place of crime. There is one of Dorothy Sayers' in which a man is murdered alone at night in his house by a mechanically released weight which works because he always turns the radio on at just such a moment, always stands in just such a position in front of it, and always bends over just so far. A couple of inches either way and the customers would get a rain check. This is what is vulgarly known as having God sit in your lap; a murderer who needs that much help from Providence must be in the wrong business.

And there is a scheme of Agatha Christie's featuring M. Hercule Poirot, that ingenious Belgian who talks in a literal translation of schoolboy French, wherein, by duly messing around with his 'little grey cells', M. Poirot decides that nobody on a certain sleeper could have done the murder alone, therefore everybody did it together, breaking the process down into a series of simple operations, like assembling an egg-beater. This is the type that is guaranteed to knock the keenest mind for a loop. Only a halfwit could guess it.

There are much better plots by these same writers and by others of their school. There may be one somewhere that would really stand up under close scrutiny. It would be fun to read it, even if I did have to go back to page 47 and refresh my memory about exactly what time the second gardener potted the prize-winning tea rose begonia. There is nothing new about these stories and nothing old. The ones I mention are all English only because the authorities (such as they are) seem to feel the English writers had an edge in this dreary routine, and that the Americans (even the creator of Philo Vance – probably the most asinine character in detective fiction) only made the Junior Varsity.

This, the classic detective story, has learned nothing and forgotten nothing. It is the story you will find almost any week in the big shiny magazines, handsomely illustrated, and paying due deference to virginal love and the right kind of luxury goods. Perhaps the tempo has become a trifle faster, and the dialogue a little more glib. There are more frozen daiquiris and stingers ordered, and fewer glasses of crusty old port; more clothes by *Vogue*, and décors by *House Beautiful*, more chic, but not more truth. We spend more time in Miami hotels and Cape Cod summer colonies and go not so often down by the old grey sundial in the Elizabethan garden.

But fundamentally it is the same careful grouping of suspects, the same utterly incomprehensible trick of how somebody stabbed Mrs Pottington Postlethwaite III with the solid platinum poniard just as she flatted on the top note of the Bell Song from Lakmé in the presence of fifteen ill-assorted guests; the same ingénue in fur-trimmed pyjamas screaming in the night to make the company pop in and out of doors and ball up the timetable; the same moody silence next day as they sit around sipping Singapore slings and sneering at each other, while the flatfeet crawl to and fro under the Persian rugs, with their derby hats on.

Personally I like the English style better. It is not quite so brittle, and the people as a rule, just wear clothes and drink drinks. There is more sense of background, as if Cheesecake Manor really existed all around and not just the part the camera sees; there are more long walks over the downs and the characters don't all try to behave as if they had just been tested by MGM. The English may not always be the best writers in the world, but they are incomparably the best dull writers.

There is a very simple statement to be made about all these stories: they do not really come off intellectually as problems, and they do not come off artistically as fiction. They are too contrived, and too little aware of what goes on in the world. They try to be honest, but honesty is an art.

The poor writer is dishonest without knowing it, and the fairly good one can be dishonest because he doesn't know what to be honest about. He thinks a complicated murder scheme which baffled the lazy reader, who won't be bothered itemizing the details, will also baffle the police, whose business is with details.

The boys with their feet on the desks know that the easiest murder case in the world to break is the one somebody tried to get very cute with; the one that really bothers them is the murder somebody only thought of two minutes before he pulled it off. But if the writers of this fiction wrote about the kind of murders that happen, they would also have to write about the authentic flavour of life as it is lived. And since they cannot do that, they pretend that what they do is what should be done. Which is begging the question – and the best of them know it.

In her introduction to the first *Omnibus of Crime*, Dorothy Sayers wrote: 'It (the detective story) does not, and by hypothesis never can, attain the loftiest level of literary achievement.' And she suggested somewhere else that this is because it is a 'literature of escape' and not 'a literature of expression'. I do not know what the loftiest level of literary achievement is: neither did Aeschylus or Shakespeare; neither does Miss Sayers. Other things being equal, which they never are, a more powerful theme will provoke a more powerful performance. Yet some very dull books have been written about God, and some very fine ones about how to make a living and stay fairly honest. It is always a matter of who writes the stuff, and what he has in him to write it with.

As for literature of expression and literature of escape, this is critics' jargon, a use of abstract words as if they had absolute meanings. Everything written with vitality expresses that vitality; there are no dull subjects, only dull minds. All men who read escape from something else into what lies behind the printed page; the quality of the dream may be argued, but its release has become a functional necessity. All men must escape at times from the deadly rhythm of their private thoughts. It is part of the process of life among thinking beings. It is one of the things that distinguish them from the three-toed sloth; he apparently – one can never be quite sure – is perfectly content hanging upside down on a branch, and not even reading Walter Lippmann. I hold no particular brief for the detective story as the ideal escape. I merely say that *all* reading for pleasure is escape, whether it be Greek, mathematics, astronomy, Benedetto Croce, or The Diary of the Forgotten Man. To say otherwise is to be an intellectual snob, and a juvenile at the art of living.

I do not think such considerations moved Miss Dorothy Sayers to her essay in critical futility.

I think what was really gnawing at her mind was the slow realization that her kind of detective story was an arid formula which could not even satisfy its own implications. It was second-grade literature because it was not about the things that could make first-grade literature. If it started out to be about real people (and she could write about them – her minor characters show that), they must very soon do unreal things in order to form the artificial pattern required by the plot. When they did unreal things, they ceased to be real themselves. They became puppets and cardboard lovers and papier-mâché villains and detectives of exquisite and impossible gentility.

The only kind of writer who could be happy with these properties was the one who did not know what reality was. Dorothy Sayers' own stories show that she was annoyed by this triteness; the weakest element in them is the part that makes them detective stories, the strongest the part which could be removed without touching the 'problem of logic and deductions'. Yet she could not or would not give her characters their heads and let them make their own mystery. It took a much simpler and more direct mind than hers to do that.

In *The Long Week-end*, which is a drastically competent account of English life and manners in the decade following the First World War, Robert Graves and Alan Hodge gave some attention to the detective story. They were just as traditionally English as the ornaments of the Golden Age, and they wrote of the time in which these writers were almost as well known as any writers in the world. Their books in one form or another sold into the millions, and in a dozen languages. These were the people who fixed the form and established the rules and founded the famous Detection Club, which is a parnassus of English writers of mystery. Its roster includes practically every important writer of detective fiction since Conan Doyle.

But Graves and Hodge decided that during this whole period only one first-class writer had written detective stories at all. An American, Dashiell Hammett. Traditional or not, Graves and Hodge were not fuddy-duddy connoisseurs of the second-rate; they could see what went on in the world and that the detective story of their time didn't; and they were aware that writers who have the vision and the ability to produce real fiction do not produce unreal fiction.

How original a writer Hammett really was, it isn't easy to decide now, even if it mattered. He was one of a group, the only one who achieved critical recognition, but not the only one who wrote or tried to write realistic mystery fiction. All literary movements are like this; some one individual is picked out to represent the whole movement; he is usually the culmination of the movement. Hammett was the ace performer, but there is nothing in his work that is not implicit in the early novels and short stories of Hemingway.

Yet for all I know, Hemingway may have learned something from Hammett, as well as from writers like Dreiser, Ring Lardner, Carl Sandburg, Sherwood Anderson and himself. A rather revolutionary debunking of both the language and material of fiction had been going on for some time. It probably started in poetry; almost everything does. You can take it clear back to Walt Whitman, if you like. But Hammett applied it to the detective story, and this, because of its heavy crust of English gentility and American pseudo-gentility, was pretty hard to get moving.

I doubt that Hammett had any deliberate artistic aims whatever; he was trying to make a living by writing something he had first-hand information about. He made some of it up; all writers do; but it had a basis in fact; it was made up out of real things. The only reality the English detection writers knew was the conversational accent of Surbiton and Bognor Regis. If they wrote about dukes and Venetian vases, they knew no more about them out of their own experience than the well-heeled Hollywood character knows about the French Modernists that hang in his Bel-Air château or the semi-antique Chippendale-cum-cobbler's-bench that he uses for a coffee table. Hammett took murder out of the Venetian vase and dropped it into the alley; it doesn't have to stay there for ever, but it was a good idea to begin by getting as far as possible from Emily Posts' idea of how a well-bred débutante gnaws a chicken wing.

Hammett wrote at first (and almost to the end) for people with a sharp, aggressive attitude to life. They were not afraid of the seamy side of things; they lived there. Violence did not dismay them; it was right down their street. Hammett gave murder back to the kind of people that commit it for reasons, not just to provide a corpse; and with the means at hand, not with handwrought duelling pistols, curare, and tropical fish. He put these people down on paper as they are, and he made them talk and think in the language they customarily used for these purposes.

He had style, but his audience didn't know it, because it was in a language not supposed to be capable of such refinements. They thought they were getting a good meaty melodrama written in the kind of lingo they imagined they spoke themselves. It was, in a sense, but it was much more. All language begins with speech, and the speech of common men at that, but when it develops to the point of becoming a literary medium it only looks like speech. Hammett's style at its worst was almost as formalized as a page of *Marius the Epicurean*; at its best it could say almost anything. I believe this style, which does not belong to Hammett or to anybody, but is the American language (and not even exclusively that any more), can say things he did not know how to say or feel the need of saying. In his hands it had no overtones, left no echo, evoked no imagine beyond a distant hill.

Hammett is said to have lacked heart, yet the story he thought most of himself is the record of a man's devotion to a friend. He was spare, frugal, hard-boiled, but he did over and over again what only the best writers can ever do at all. He wrote scenes that seemed never to have been written before.

With all this he did not wreck the formal detective story. Nobody can; production demands a form that can be produced. Realism takes too much talent, too much knowledge, too much awareness. Hammett may have loosened it up a little here, and sharpened it a little there. Certainly all but the stupidest and most meretricious writers are more conscious of their artificiality than they used to be. And he demonstrated that the detective story can be important writing. *The Maltese Falcon* may or may not be a work of genius, but an art which is capable of it is not 'by hypothesis' incapable of anything. Once a detective story can be as good as this, only the pedants will deny that it *could* be even better.

Hammett did something else, he made the detective story fun to write, not an exhausting concatenation of insignificant clues. Without him there might not have been a regional mystery as clever as Percival Wilde's *Inquest*, or an ironic study as able as Raymond Postgate's *Verdict of Twelve*, or a savage piece of intellectual double-talk like Kenneth Fearing's *The Dagger of the Mind*, or a tragi-comic idealization of the murderer as in Donald Henderson's *Mr Bowling Buys a Newspaper*, or even a gay and intriguing Hollywoodian gambol like Richard Sale's *Lazarus No. 7*.

The realistic style is easy to abuse: from haste, from lack of awareness, from inability to bridge the chasm that lies between what a writer would like to be able to say and what he actually knows how to say. It is easy to fake; brutality is not strength, flipness is not wit, edge-of-the-chair writing can be as boring as flat writing; dalliance with promiscuous blondes can be very dull stuff when described by goaty young men with no other purpose in mind than to describe dalliance with promiscuous blondes. There has been so much of this sort of thing that if a character in a detective story says 'Yeah,' the author is automatically a Hammett imitator.

And there are still quite a few people around who say that Hammett did not write detective stories at all, merely hard-boiled chronicles of mean streets with a perfunctory mystery element dropped in like the olive in a martini. These are the flustered old ladies – of both sexes (or no sex) and almost all ages – who like their murders scented with magnolia blossoms and do not care to be reminded that murder is an act of infinite cruelty, even if the perpetrators sometimes look like playboys or college professors or nice motherly women with softly greying hair.

There are also a few badly scared champions of the formal or the classic mystery who thinks no story is a detective story which does not pose a formal and exact problem and arrange the clues around it with neat labels on them. Such would point out, for example, that in reading *The Maltese Falcon* no one concerns himself with who killed Spade's partner, Archer (which is the only formal probem of the story), because the reader is kept thinking about something else. Yet in *The Glass Key* the reader is constantly reminded that the question is who killed Taylor Henry, and exactly the same effect is obtained; an effect of movement, intrigue, cross-purposes and the gradual elucidation of character, which is all the detective story has any right to be about anyway. The rest is spillikins in the parlour.

But all this (and Hammett too) is for me not quite enough. The realist in murder writes of a world in which gangsters can rule nations and almost rule cities, in which hotels and apartment houses and celebrated restaurants are owned by men who made their money out of brothels, in which a screen star can be the finger man for a mob, and the nice man down the hall is a boss of the numbers racket; a world where a judge with a cellar full of bootleg liquor can send a man to jail for having a pint in his pocket, where the mayor of your town may have condoned murder as an instrument of money-making, where no man can walk down a dark street in safety because law and order are things we talk about but refrain from practising; a world where you may witness a hold-up in broad daylight and see who did it, but you will fade quickly back into the crowd rather than tell anyone, because the hold-up men may have friends with long guns, or the police may not like your testimony, and in any case the shyster for the defence will be allowed to abuse and vilify you in open court, before a jury of selected morons, without any but the most perfunctory interference from a political judge.

It is not a very fragrant world, but it is the world you live in, and certain writers with tough minds and a cool spirit of detachment can make very interesting and even amusing patterns out of it. It is not funny that a man should be killed, but it is sometimes funny that he should be killed for so little, and that his death should be the coin of what we call civilization. All this still is not quite enough.

In everything that can be called art there is a quality of redemption. It may be pure tragedy, if it is high tragedy, and it may be pity and irony, and it may be the raucous laughter of the strong man. But down these mean streets a man must go who is not himself mean, who is neither tarnished nor afraid. The detective in this kind of story must be such a man. He is the hero, he is everything. He must be a complete man and a common man and yet an unusual man. He must be, to use a rather weathered phrase, a man of honour, by instinct, by inevitability, without thought of it, and certainly without saying it. He must be the best man in his world and a good enough man for any world. I do not care much about his private life; he is neither a eunuch nor a satyr; I think he might seduce a duchess and I am quite sure he would not spoil a virgin; if he is a man of honour in one thing, he is that in all things.

He is a relatively poor man, or he would not be a detective

at all. He is a common man or he could not go among common people. He has a sense of character, or he would not know his job. He will take no man's money dishonestly and no man's insolence without a due and dispassionate revenge. He is a lonely man and his pride is that you will treat him as a proud man or be very sorry you ever saw him. He talks as the man of his age talks, that is, with rude wit, a lively sense of the grotesque, a disgust for sham, and a contempt for pettiness.

The story is this man's adventure in search of a hidden truth, and it would be no adventure if it did not happen to a man fit for adventure. He has a range of awareness that startles you, but it belongs to him by right, because it belongs to the world he lives in. If there were enough like him, I think the world would be a very safe place to live in, and yet not too dull to be worth living in.

Ed McBain

Heat £2.50

In the heat of the city summer, Jerry Newman, failed painter and twice-failed husband, died. Suicide they said, but Carella knew that suicides left notes and didn't turn the air-conditioning off on the hottest night of the year. Which puts Carella on the trail of a killer, while Kling's on the trail of a lovely wife he can't trust, and someone nasty is on Kling's trail.

'Tense, gripping and stylish . . . by the best modern American crime writer' SUNDAY EXPRESS

Ice £2.50

It was snowing again on the frozen sidewalks when the girl dancer walked out of the stage door and straight into the gunsight of the man hidden in the nearby doorway. When they pulled the .38 Smith & Wesson slug out of her corpse, Ballistics noticed that it matched the one they'd found in a Puerto Rican dope dealer just three days before. Carella knew which direction he was taking. Ice means winter on the Precinct streets, and ice means killing. But ice means something else too, something every bit as deadly . . .

Jigsaw £1.75

There's nothing like a little homicide to give the 87th Precinct a shot in the arm. Or the chest, as the case may be . . . Detectives Brown and Carella had themselves a puzzle with six missing pieces. Put it together and there's $750,000 for the taking. In this case bodies were easy to find – clues came a little harder . . .

'McBain's so far ahead of police-procedural writers that its virtually a one-horse race . . . Hyper-readable, witty, credible' SCOTSMAN

Raymond Chandler

The Little Sister £1.95

When she walked into Marlowe's office she looked just like the pathetic but appealing small-town girl from Manhattan. Manhattan, Kansas. He sensed something phoney about her. Prissy-looking, provincial, anxious about her missing brother . . . but there was still something strangely phoney . . .

The High Window £1.95

'Mrs Elizabeth Bright Murdock and family wanted to hire a nice clean private detective who wouldn't drop cigar ashes on the floor and never carried more than one gun . . .'

Marlowe met Mrs Murdock on a hot afternoon in her palatial residence. She had jet buttons in her ears and a bottle of port on the side table. Marlowe didn't drink port in hot weather. Just as well. Mrs Murdock didn't offer him any. In addition to the bottle and the buttons, Mrs Murdock had a secretary. Quiet sort. Scared three parts out of her wits. All of which launched Marlowe into the case of the Brasher Doubloon – a very rare gold coin indeed. Rare enough to turn Marlowe's job into a murder case . . .